GAMES AT TWILIGHT

Anita Desai was born and educated in India. Her
published works include novels, children's books and
short stories. *Clear Light of Day* (1980), *In Custody*
(1984) and *Fasting, Feasting* (1999) were all shortlisted
for the Booker Prize, and *The Village by the Sea* won
the *Guardian* Award for Children's Fiction in 1982.
Anita Desai is a Fellow of the Royal Society of
Literature in London, of the American Academy of
Arts and Letters in New York and of Girton College at
the University of Cambridge. She teaches in the Writing
Program at M.I.T. and divides her time between India,
Boston, Massachusetts and Cambridge, England. *In
Custody* was recently filmed by Merchant Ivory
Productions.

BY ANITA DESAI

Anita Desai

GAMES AT TWILIGHT

and other stories

VINTAGE

Published by Vintage 1998

4 6 8 10 9 7 5 3

Copyright © Anita Desai 1978

The right of Anita Desai to be identified as the author of
this work has been asserted by him in accordance with the
Copyright, Designs and Patents Act, 1988

This book is sold subject to the condition that it shall not,
by way of trade or otherwise, be lent, resold, hired out, or
otherwise circulated without the publisher's prior consent
in any form of binding or cover other than that in which it
is published and without a similar condition including this
condition being imposed on the subsequent purchaser

First published in Great Britain by
William Heinemann Ltd 1978

Surface Textures' first appeared in
Macmillan's *Winter Tales* no. 23

Vintage
Random House, 20 Vauxhall Bridge Road,
London SW1V 2SA

Random House Australia (Pty) Limited
20 Alfred Street, Milsons Point, Sydney,
New South Wales 2061, Australia

Random House New Zealand Limited
18 Poland Road, Glenfield,
Auckland 10, New Zealand

Random House (Pty) Limited
Endulini, 5a Jubilee Road, Parktown 2193,
South Africa

The Random House Group Limited Reg. No. 954009

www.randomhouse.co.uk

A CIP catalogue record for this book
is available from the British Library

ISBN 0 09 942853 9

Papers used by Random House are natural, recyclable
products made from wood grown in sustainable forests.
The manufacturing processes conform to the environ-
mental regulations of the country of origin.

Printed and bound in Great Britain by
Cox & Wyman Ltd, Reading, Berkshire

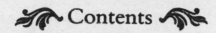 Contents

For Dada

Games at Twilight

It was still too hot to play outdoors. They had had their tea, they had been washed and had their hair brushed, and after the long day of confinement in the house that was not cool but at least a protection from the sun, the children strained to get out. Their faces were red and bloated with the effort, but their mother would not open the door, everything was still curtained and shuttered in a way that stifled the children, made them feel that their lungs were stuffed with cotton wool and their noses with dust and if they didn't burst out into the light and see the sun and feel the air, they would choke.

'Please, ma, please,' they begged. 'We'll play in the veranda and porch – we won't go a step out of the porch.'

'You will, I know you will, and then—'

'No – we won't, we won't,' they wailed so horrendously that she actually let down the bolt of the front door so that they burst out like seeds from a crackling, over-ripe pod into the veranda, with such wild, maniacal yells that she retreated to her bath and the shower of talcum powder and the fresh sari that were to help her face the summer evening.

They faced the afternoon. It was too hot. Too bright. The

1

white walls of the veranda glared stridently in the sun. The bougainvillea hung about it, purple and magenta, in livid balloons. The garden outside was like a tray made of beaten brass, flattened out on the red gravel and the stony soil in all shades of metal – aluminium, tin, copper and brass. No life stirred at this arid time of day – the birds still drooped, like dead fruit, in the papery tents of the trees; some squirrels lay limp on the wet earth under the garden tap. The outdoor dog lay stretched as if dead on the veranda mat, his paws and ears and tail all reaching out like dying travellers in search of water. He rolled his eyes at the children – two white marbles rolling in the purple sockets, begging for sympathy – and attempted to lift his tail in a wag but could not. It only twitched and lay still.

Then, perhaps roused by the shrieks of the children, a band of parrots suddenly fell out of the eucalyptus tree, tumbled frantically in the still, sizzling air, then sorted themselves out into battle formation and streaked away across the white sky.

The children, too, felt released. They too began tumbling, shoving, pushing against each other, frantic to start. Start what? Start their business. The business of the children's day which is – play.

'Let's play hide-and-seek.'

'Who'll be It?'

'You be It.'

'Why should I? You be—'

'You're the eldest—'

'That doesn't mean—'

The shoves became harder. Some kicked out. The motherly Mira intervened. She pulled the boys roughly apart. There was a tearing sound of cloth but it was lost in the heavy panting and angry grumbling and no one paid attention to the small sleeve hanging loosely off a shoulder.

'Make a circle, make a circle!' she shouted, firmly pulling and pushing till a kind of vague circle was formed. 'Now clap!' she roared and, clapping, they all chanted in melancholy unison: 'Dip, dip, dip – my blue ship—' and every now and then one or the other saw he was safe by the way his hands fell at the crucial moment – palm on palm, or back of hand on palm – and dropped out of the circle with a yell and a jump of relief and jubilation.

Raghu was It. He started to protest, to cry 'You cheated – Mira cheated – Anu cheated—' but it was too late, the others had all already streaked away. There was no one to hear when he called out, 'Only in the veranda – the porch – Ma said – Ma *said* to stay in the porch!' No one had stopped to listen, all he saw were their brown legs flashing through the dusty shrubs, scrambling up brick walls, leaping over compost heaps and hedges, and then the porch stood empty in the purple shade of the bougainvillea and the garden was as empty as before; even the limp squirrels had whisked away, leaving everything gleaming, brassy and bare.

Only small Manu suddenly reappeared, as if he had dropped out of an invisible cloud or from a bird's claws, and stood for a moment in the centre of the yellow lawn, chewing his finger and near to tears as he heard Raghu shouting, with his head pressed against the veranda wall, 'Eighty-three, eighty-five, eighty-nine, ninety...' and then made off in a panic, half of him wanting to fly north, the other half counselling south. Raghu turned just in time to see the flash of his white shorts and the uncertain skittering of his red sandals, and charged after him with such a bloodcurdling yell that Manu stumbled over the hosepipe, fell into its rubber coils and lay there weeping, 'I won't be It – you have to find them all – all – All!'

'I know I have to, idiot,' Raghu said, superciliously kicking him with his toe. 'You're dead,' he said with satisfaction, licking the beads of perspiration off his upper lip, and then stalked off in search of worthier prey, whistling spiritedly so that the hiders should hear and tremble.

Ravi heard the whistling and picked his nose in a panic, trying to find comfort by burrowing the finger deep–deep into that soft tunnel. He felt himself too exposed, sitting on an upturned flower pot behind the garage. Where could he burrow? He could run around the garage if he heard Raghu come – around and around and around – but he hadn't much faith in his short legs when matched against Raghu's long, hefty, hairy footballer legs. Ravi had a frightening glimpse of them as Raghu combed the hedge of crotons and hibiscus, trampling delicate ferns underfoot as he did so. Ravi looked about him desperately, swallowing a small ball of snot in his fear.

The garage was locked with a great heavy lock to which the driver had the key in his room, hanging from a nail on the wall under his work–shirt. Ravi had peeped in and seen him still sprawling on his string–cot in his vest and striped underpants, the hair on his chest and the hair in his nose shaking with the vibrations of his phlegm–obstructed snores. Ravi had wished he were tall enough, big enough to reach the key on the nail, but it was impossible, beyond his reach for years to come. He had sidled away and sat dejectedly on the flower pot. That at least was cut to his own size.

But next to the garage was another shed with a big green door. Also locked. No one even knew who had the key to the lock. That shed wasn't opened more than once a year when Ma turned out all the old broken bits of furniture and rolls of matting and leaking buckets, and the white ant hills were broken and swept away and Flit sprayed into the spider webs and rat holes so that the whole operation was like the looting of a poor, ruined and conquered city. The green leaves of the door sagged. They were nearly off their rusty hinges. The hinges were large and made a small gap

4

between the door and the walls – only just large enough for rats, dogs and, possibly, Ravi to slip through.

Ravi had never cared to enter such a dark and depressing mortuary of defunct household goods seething with such unspeakable and alarming animal life but, as Raghu's whistling grew angrier and sharper and his crashing and storming in the hedge wilder, Ravi suddenly slipped off the flower pot and through the crack and was gone. He chuckled aloud with astonishment at his own temerity so that Raghu came out of the hedge, stood silent with his hands on his hips, listening, and finally shouted 'I heard you! I'm coming! *Got* you—' and came charging round the garage only to find the upturned flower pot, the yellow dust, the crawling of white ants in a mud-hill against the closed shed door – nothing. Snarling, he bent to pick up a stick and went off, whacking it against the garage and shed walls as if to beat out his prey.

Ravi shook, then shivered with delight, with self-congratulation. Also with fear. It was dark, spooky in the shed. It had a muffled smell, as of graves. Ravi had once got locked into the linen cupboard and sat there weeping for half an hour before he was rescued. But at least that had been a familiar place, and even smelt pleasantly of starch, laundry and, reassuringly, of his mother. But the shed smelt of rats, ant hills, dust and spider webs. Also of less definable, less recognizable horrors. And it was dark. Except for the white-hot cracks along the door, there was no light. The roof was very low. Although Ravi was small, he felt as if he could reach up and touch it with his finger tips. But he didn't stretch. He hunched himself into a ball so as not to bump into anything, touch or feel anything. What might there not be to touch him and feel him as he stood there, trying to see in the dark? Something cold, or slimy – like a snake. Snakes! He leapt up as Raghu whacked the wall with

5

his stick – then, quickly realizing what it was, felt almost relieved to hear Raghu, hear his stick. It made him feel protected.

But Raghu soon moved away. There wasn't a sound once his footsteps had gone around the garage and disappeared. Ravi stood frozen inside the shed. Then he shivered all over. Something had tickled the back of his neck. It took him a while to pick up the courage to lift his hand and explore. It was an insect – perhaps a spider – exploring *him*. He squashed it and wondered how many more creatures were watching him, waiting to reach out and touch him, the stranger.

There was nothing now. After standing in that position – his hand still on his neck, feeling the wet splodge of the squashed spider gradually dry – for minutes, hours, his legs began to tremble with the effort, the inaction. By now he could see enough in the dark to make out the large solid shapes of old wardrobes, broken buckets and bedsteads piled on top of each other around him. He recognized an old bathtub – patches of enamel glimmered at him and at last he lowered himself onto its edge.

He contemplated slipping out of the shed and into the fray. He wondered if it would not be better to be captured by Raghu and be returned to the milling crowd as long as he could be in the sun, the light, the free spaces of the garden and the familiarity of his brothers, sisters and cousins. It would be evening soon. Their games would become legitimate. The parents would sit out on the lawn on cane basket chairs and watch them as they tore around the garden or gathered in knots to share a loot of mulberries or black, teeth-splitting *jamun* from the garden trees. The gardener would fix the hosepipe to the water tap and water would fall lavishly through the air to the ground, soaking the dry yellow grass and the red gravel and arousing the sweet, the intoxicating scent of water on dry earth – that loveliest scent in the world. Ravi sniffed for a whiff of it. He half-rose from the bathtub, then heard the despairing scream of one of the girls as Raghu bore down upon her. There was the sound of a crash, and of rolling about in the bushes, the shrubs, then screams and accusing sobs of, 'I touched the den—' 'You did not—' 'I did—' 'You liar, you did *not*' and then a fading away and silence again.

Ravi sat back on the harsh edge of the tub, deciding to hold out a bit longer. What fun if they were all found and caught – he alone left unconquered! He had never known that sensation. Nothing more wonderful had ever happened to him than being taken out by an uncle and bought a whole slab of chocolate all to himself, or being flung into the soda-man's pony cart and driven up to the gate by the friendly driver with the red beard and pointed ears. To defeat Raghu – that hirsute, hoarse-voiced football champion – and to be the winner in a circle of older, bigger, luckier children – that would be thrilling beyond imagination. He hugged his knees together and smiled to himself almost shyly at the thought of so much victory, such laurels.

There he sat smiling, knocking his heels against the bathtub, now and then getting up and going to the door to put his ear to the broad crack and listening for sounds of the game, the pursuer and the pursued, and then returning to his seat with the dogged determination of the true winner, a breaker of records, a champion.

It grew darker in the shed as the light at the door grew softer, fuzzier, turned to a kind of crumbling yellow pollen that turned to yellow fur, blue fur, grey fur. Evening. Twilight. The sound of water gushing, falling. The scent of earth receiving water, slaking its thirst in great gulps and releasing that green scent of freshness, coolness. Through the crack Ravi saw the long purple shadows of the shed and the garage lying still across the yard. Beyond that, the white walls of the house. The bougainvillea had lost its lividity, hung in dark bundles that quaked and twittered and seethed with masses of homing sparrows. The lawn was shut off from his view. Could he hear the children's voices? It seemed to him that he could. It seemed to him that he could hear them chanting, singing, laughing. But what about the game? What had happened? Could it be over? How could it when he was still not found?

It then occurred to him that he could have slipped out long ago, dashed across the yard to the veranda and touched the 'den'. It was necessary to do that to win. He had forgotten. He had only remembered the part of hiding and trying to elude the seeker. He had done that so successfully, his success had occupied him so wholly that he had quite forgotten that success had to be clinched by that final dash to victory and the ringing cry of 'Den!'

With a whimper he burst through the crack, fell on his knees, got up and stumbled on stiff, benumbed legs across the shadowy yard, crying heartily by the time he reached the veranda so that when he flung himself at the white pillar and bawled, 'Den! Den! Den!' his voice broke with rage and pity at the disgrace of it all and he felt himself flooded with tears and misery.

Out on the lawn, the children stopped chanting. They all turned to stare at him in amazement. Their faces were pale and triangular in the dusk. The trees and bushes around them stood inky and sepulchral, spilling long shadows across them. They stared, wondering at his reappearance, his passion, his wild animal howling. Their mother rose from her basket chair and came towards him, worried, annoyed, saying, 'Stop it, stop it, Ravi. Don't be a baby. Have you hurt yourself?' Seeing him attended to, the children went back to clasping their hands and chanting 'The grass is green, the rose is red. . . .'

But Ravi would not let them. He tore himself out of his

mother's grasp and pounded across the lawn into their midst, charging at them with his head lowered so that they scattered in surprise. 'I won, I won, I won,' he bawled, shaking his head so that the big tears flew. 'Raghu didn't find me. I won, I won—'

It took them a minute to grasp what he was saying, even who he was. They had quite forgotten him. Raghu had found all the others long ago. There had been a fight about who was to be It next. It had been so fierce that their mother had emerged from her bath and made them change to another game. Then they had played another and another. Broken mulberries from the tree and eaten them. Helped the driver wash the car when their father returned from work. Helped the gardener water the beds till he roared at them and swore he would complain to their parents. The parents had come out, taken up their positions on the cane chairs. They had begun to play again, sing and chant. All this time no one had remembered Ravi. Having disappeared from the scene, he had disappeared from their minds. Clean.

'Don't be a fool,' Raghu said roughly, pushing him aside, and even Mira said, 'Stop howling, Ravi. If you want to play, you can stand at the end of the line,' and she put him there very firmly.

The game proceeded. Two pairs of arms reached up and met in an arc. The children trooped under it again and again in a lugubrious circle, ducking their heads and intoning

'The grass is green,
The rose is red;
Remember me
When I am dead, dead, dead, dead . . .'

And the arc of thin arms trembled in the twilight, and the heads were bowed so sadly, and their feet tramped to that melancholy refrain so mournfully, so helplessly, that Ravi could not bear it. He would not follow them, he would not

9

be included in this funereal game. He had wanted victory and triumph – not a funeral. But he had been forgotten, left out and he would not join them now. The ignominy of being forgotten – how could he face it? He felt his heart go heavy and ache inside him unbearably. He lay down full length on the damp grass, crushing his face into it, no longer crying, silenced by a terrible sense of his insignificance.

Private Tuition by Mr Bose

Mr Bose gave his private tuition out on the balcony, in the evenings, in the belief that, since it faced south, the river Hooghly would send it a wavering breeze or two to drift over the rooftops, through the washing and the few pots of *tulsi* and marigold that his wife had placed precariously on the balcony rail, to cool him, fan him, soothe him. But there was no breeze: it was hot, the air hung upon them like a damp towel, gagging him and, speaking through this gag, he tiredly intoned the Sanskrit verses that should, he felt, have been roared out on a hill-top at sunrise.

'*Aum. Usa va asvasya medhyasya sirah . . .*'

It came out, of course, a mumble. Asked to translate, his pupil, too, scowled as he had done, thrust his fist through his hair and mumbled:

'Aum is the dawn and the head of a horse . . .'

Mr Bose protested in a low wail. 'What horse, my boy? What horse?'

The boy rolled his eyes sullenly. 'I don't know, sir, it doesn't say.'

Mr Bose looked at him in disbelief. He was the son of a Brahmin priest who himself instructed him in the Maha-bharata all morning, turning him over to Mr Bose only

11

in the evening when he set out to officiate at weddings, *puja*
and other functions for which he was so much in demand on
account of his stately bearing, his calm and inscrutable face
and his sensuous voice that so suited the Sanskrit language
in which he, almost always, discoursed. And this was his
son – this Pritam with his red-veined eyes and oiled locks,
his stumbling fingers and shuffling feet that betrayed his
secret life, its scruffiness, its gutters and drains full of
resentment and destruction. Mr Bose suddenly remembered how he had seen him, from the window of a bus that
had come to a standstill on the street due to a fist fight
between the conductor and a passenger, Pritam slipping up
the stairs, through the door, into a neon-lit bar off Park
Street.

'The sacrificial horse,' Mr Bose explained with forced
patience. 'Have you heard of Asvamedha, Pritam, the royal
horse that was let loose to run through the kingdom before
it returned to the capital and was sacrificed by the king?'

The boy gave him a look of such malice that Mr Bose bit
the end of his moustache and fell silent, shuffling through
the pages. 'Read on, then,' he mumbled and listened, for a
while, as Pritam blundered heavily through the Sanskrit
verses that rolled off his father's experienced tongue, and
even Mr Bose's shy one, with such rich felicity. When he
could not bear it any longer, he turned his head, slightly,
just enough to be able to look out of the corner of his eye
through the open door, down the unlit passage at the end of
which, in the small, dimly lit kitchen, his wife sat kneading
dough for bread, their child at her side. Her head was bowed
so that some of her hair had freed itself of the long steel pins
he hated so much and hung about her pale, narrow face. The
red border of her sari was the only stripe of colour in that
smoky scene. The child beside her had his back turned to the
door so that Mr Bose could see his little brown buttocks
under the short white shirt, squashed firmly down upon the

woven mat. Mr Bose wondered what it was that kept him so quiet – perhaps his mother had given him a lump of dough to mould into some thick and satisfying shape. Both of them seemed bound together and held down in some deeply absorbing act from which he was excluded. He would have liked to break in and join them.

Pritam stopped reading, maliciously staring at Mr Bose whose lips were wavering into a smile beneath the ragged moustache. The woman, disturbed by the break in the recitation on the balcony, looked up, past the child, down the passage and into Mr Bose's face. Mr Bose's moustache lifted up like a pair of wings and, beneath them, his smile lifted up and out with almost a laugh of tenderness and delight. Beginning to laugh herself, she quickly turned, pulled down the corners of her mouth with mock sternness, trying to recall him to the path of duty, and picking up a lump of sticky dough, handed it back to the child, softly urging him to be quiet and let his father finish the lesson.

Pritam, the scabby, oil-slick son of a Brahmin priest, coughed theatrically – a cough imitating that of a favourite screen actor, surely, it was so false and over-done and suggestive. Mr Bose swung around in dismay, crying 'Why have you stopped? Go on, go on.'

'You weren't listening, sir.'

Many words, many questions leapt to Mr Bose's lips, ready to pounce on this miserable boy whom he could hardly bear to see sitting beneath his wife's holy *tulsi* plant that she tended with prayers, water-can and oil-lamp every evening. Then, growing conscious of the way his moustache was agitating upon his upper lip, he said only, 'Read.

'*Ahar va asvam purustan mahima nvajagata . . .*'

Across the road someone turned on a radio and a song filled with a pleasant, lilting *weltschmerz* twirled and sank, twirled and rose from that balcony to this. Pritam raised his voice, grinding through the Sanskrit consonants like some

13

dying, diseased tram-car. From the kitchen only a murmur and the soft thumping of the dough in the pan could be heard – sounds as soft and comfortable as sleepy pigeons'. Mr Bose longed passionately to listen to them, catch every faintest nuance of them, but to do this he would have to smash the radio, hurl the Brahmin's son down the iron stairs . . . He curled up his hands on his knees and drew his feet together under him, horrified at this welling up of violence inside him, under his pale pink bush-shirt, inside his thin, ridiculously heaving chest. As often as Mr Bose longed to alter the entire direction of the world's revolution, as often as he longed to break the world apart into two halves and shake out of them – what? Festival fireworks, a woman's soft hair, blood-stained feathers? – he would shudder and pale at the thought of his indiscretion, his violence, this secret force that now and then threatened, clamoured, so that he had quickly to still it, squash it. After all, he must continue with his private tuitions: that was what was important. The baby had to have his first pair of shoes and soon he would be needing oranges, biscuits, plastic toys. 'Read,' said Mr Bose, a little less sternly, a little more sadly.

But, 'It is seven, I can go home now,' said Pritam triumphantly, throwing his father's thick yellow Mahabharata into his bag, knocking the bag shut with one fist and preparing to fly. Where did he fly to? Mr Bose wondered if it would be the neon-lit bar off Park Street. Then, seeing the boy disappear down the black stairs – the bulb had fused again – he felt it didn't matter, didn't matter one bit since it left him alone to turn, plunge down the passage and fling himself at the doorposts of the kitchen, there to stand and gaze down at his wife, now rolling out *purees* with an exquisite, back-and-forth rolling motion of her hands, and his son, trying now to make a spoon stand on one end.

She only glanced at him, pretended not to care, pursed

14

her lips to keep from giggling, flipped the *puree* over and rolled it finer and flatter still. He wanted so much to touch her hair, the strand that lay over her shoulder in a black loop, and did not know how to – she was so busy. 'Your hair is coming loose,' he said.

'Go, go,' she warned, 'I hear the next one coming.'

So did he, he heard the soft patting of sandals on the worn steps outside, so all he did was bend and touch the small curls of hair on his son's neck. They were so soft, they seemed hardly human and quite frightened him. When he took his hand away he felt the wisps might have come off onto his fingers and he rubbed the tips together wonderingly. The child let fall the spoon, with a magnificent ring, onto a brass dish and started at this discovery of percussion.

The light on the balcony was dimmed as his next pupil came to stand in the doorway. Quickly he pulled himself away from the doorpost and walked back to his station, tense with unspoken words and unexpressed emotion. He had quite forgotten that his next pupil, this Wednesday, was to be Upneet. Rather Pritam again than this once-a-week typhoon, Upneet of the flowered sari, ruby ear-rings and shaming laughter. Under this Upneet's gaze such ordinary functions of a tutor's life as sitting down at a table, sharpening a pencil and opening a book to the correct page became matters of farce, disaster and hilarity. His very bones sprang out of joint. He did not know where to look – everywhere were Upneet's flowers, Upneet's giggles. Immediately, at the very sight of the tip of her sandal peeping out beneath the flowered hem of her sari, he was a man broken to pieces, flung this way and that, rattling. Rattling.

Throwing away the Sanskrit books, bringing out volumes of Bengali poetry, opening to a poem by Jibanandan Das, he wondered ferociously: Why did she come? What use had she for Bengali poetry? Why did she come from that house across the road where the loud radio rollicked, to sit on his balcony, in view of his shy wife, making him read poetry to her? It was intolerable. Intolerable, all of it – except, only for the seventy-five rupees paid at the end of the month. Oranges, he thought grimly, and milk, medicines, clothes. And he read to her:

'Her hair was the dark night of Vidisha,
Her face the sculpture of Svarasti . . .'

Quite steadily he read, his tongue tamed and enthralled by the rhythm of the verse he had loved (copied on a sheet of blue paper, he had sent it to his wife one day when speech proved inadequate).

' "Where have you been so long?" she asked,
Lifting her bird's-nest eyes,
Banalata Sen of Natore.'

Pat-pat-pat. No, it was not the rhythm of the verse, he realized, but the tapping of her foot, green-sandalled, red-nailed, swinging and swinging to lift the hem of her sari up and up. His eyes slid off the book, watched the flowered hem swing out and up, out and up as the green-sandalled foot peeped out, then in, peeped out, then in. For a while his tongue ran on of its own volition:

'All birds come home, and all rivers,
Life's ledger is closed . . . '

But he could not continue – it was the foot, the sandal that carried on the rhythm exactly as if he were still reciting. Even the radio stopped its rollicking and, as a peremptory voice began to enumerate the day's disasters and achievements all over the world, Mr Bose heard more vigorous sounds from his kitchen as well. There too the lulling pigeon sounds had been crisply turned off and what he

16

heard were bangs and rattles among the kitchen pots, a kettledrum of commands, he thought. The baby, letting out a wail of surprise, paused, heard the nervous commotion continue and intensify and launched himself on a series of wails.

Mr Bose looked up, aghast. He could not understand how these two halves of the difficult world that he had been holding so carefully together, sealing them with reams of poetry, reams of Sanskrit, had split apart into dissonance. He stared at his pupil's face, creamy, feline, satirical, and was forced to complete the poem in a stutter:

> 'Only darkness remains, to sit facing
> Banalata Sen of Natore.'

But the darkness was filled with hideous sounds of business and anger and command. The radio news commentator barked, the baby wailed, the kitchen pots clashed. He even heard his wife's voice raised, angrily, at the child, like a threatening stick. Glancing again at his pupil whom he feared so much, he saw precisely that lift of the eyebrows and that twist of a smile that disjointed him, rattled him.

'Er – please read,' he tried to correct, to straighten that twist of eyebrows and lips. 'Please read.'

'But you have read it to me already,' she laughed, mocking him with her eyes and laugh.

'The next poem,' he cried, 'read the next poem,' and turned the page with fingers as clumsy as toes.

'It is much better when you read to me,' she complained impertinently, but read, keeping time to the rhythm with that restless foot which he watched as though it were a snake-charmer's pipe, swaying. He could hear her voice no more than the snake could the pipe's – it was drowned out by the baby's wails, swelling into roars of self-pity and indignation in this suddenly hard-edged world.

Mr Bose threw a piteous, begging look over his shoulder

17

at the kitchen. Catching his eye, his wife glowered at him, tossed the hair out of her face and cried, 'Be quiet, be quiet, can't you see how busy your father is?' Red-eared, he turned to find Upneet looking curiously down the passage at this scene of domestic anarchy, and said, 'I'm sorry, sorry – please read.'

'I have read!' she exclaimed. 'Didn't you hear me?'

'So much noise – I'm sorry,' he gasped and rose to hurry down the passage and hiss, pressing his hands to his head as he did so, 'Keep him quiet, can't you? Just for half an hour!'

'He is hungry,' his wife said, as if she could do nothing about that.

'Feed him then,' he begged.

'It isn't time,' she said angrily.

'Never mind. Feed him, feed him.'

'Why? So that you can read poetry to that girl in peace?'

'Shh!' he hissed, shocked, alarmed that Upneet would hear. His chest filled with the injustice of it. But this was no time for pleas or reason. He gave another desperate look at the child who lay crouched on the kitchen floor, rolling with misery. When he turned to go back to his pupil who was watching them interestedly, he heard his wife snatch up the child and tell him, 'Have your food then, have it and eat it – don't you see how angry your father is?'

He spent the remaining half-hour with Upneet trying to distract her from observation of his domestic life. Why should it interest her? he thought angrily. She came here to study, not to mock, not to make trouble. He was her tutor, not her clown! Sternly, he gave her dictation but she was so hopeless – she learnt no Bengali at her convent school, found it hard even to form the letters of the Bengali alphabet – that he was left speechless. He crossed out her errors with his red pencil – grateful to be able to cancel out, so effectively, some of the ugliness of his life – till there was hardly a word left uncrossed and, looking up to see her reaction, found her far less perturbed than he. In fact, she looked quite mischievously pleased. Three months of Bengali lessons to end in this! She was as truimphant as he was horrified. He let fall the red pencil with a discouraged gesture. So, in complete discord, the lesson broke apart, they all broke apart and for a while Mr Bose was alone on the balcony, clutching at the rails, thinking that these bars of cooled iron were all that were left for him to hold. Inside all was a conflict of shame and despair, in garbled grammar.

But, gradually, the grammar rearranged itself according to rule, corrected itself. The composition into quiet made quite clear the exhaustion of the child, asleep or nearly so. The sounds of dinner being prepared were calm, decorative even. Once more the radio was tuned to music, sympathetically sad. When his wife called him in to eat, he turned to go with his shoulders beaten, sagging, an attitude repeated by his moustache.

'He is asleep,' she said, glancing at him with a rather ashamed face, conciliatory.

He nodded and sat down before his brass tray. She straightened it nervously, waved a hand over it as if to drive away a fly he could not see, and turned to the fire to fry hot *purees* for him, one by one, turning quickly to heap them on his tray so fast that he begged her to stop.

'Eat more,' she coaxed. 'One more' – as though the extra *puree* were a peace offering following her rebellion of half an hour ago.

He took it with reluctant fingers but his moustache began to quiver on his lip as if beginning to wake up. 'And you?' he asked. 'Won't you eat now?'

About her mouth, too, some quivers began to rise and move. She pursed her lips, nodded and began to fill her tray, piling up the *purees* in a low stack.

'One more,' he told her, 'just one more,' he teased, and they laughed.

19

Studies in the Park

—Turn it off, turn it off, turn it off! First he listens to the
news in Hindi. Directly after, in English. Broom – brroom
– brrroom – the voice of doom roars. Next, in Tamil. Then
in Punjabi. In Gujarati. What next, my god, what next?
Turn it off before I smash it onto his head, fling it out of the
window, do nothing of the sort of course, nothing of the
sort.

—And my mother. She cuts and fries, cuts and fries. All
day I hear her chopping and slicing and the pan of oil
hissing. What all does she find to fry and feed us on, for
God's sake? Eggplants, potatoes, spinach, shoe soles, newspapers, finally she'll slice me and feed me to my brothers
and sisters. Ah, now she's turned on the tap. It's roaring and
pouring, pouring and roaring into a bucket without a
bottom.

—The bell rings. Voices clash, clatter and break. The
tin-and-bottle man? The neighbours? The police? The
Help-the-Blind man? Thieves and burglars? All of them, all
of them, ten or twenty or a hundred of them, marching up
the stairs, hammering at the door, breaking in and climbing
over me – ten, twenty or a hundred of them.

—Then, worst of all, the milk arrives. In the tallest glass

20

in the house. 'Suno, drink your milk. Good for you, Suno. You need it. Now, before the exams. Must have it, Suno. Drink.' The voice wheedles its way into my ear like a worm. I shudder. The table tips over. The milk runs. The tumbler clangs on the floor. 'Suno, Suno, how will you do your exams?'

—That is precisely what I ask myself. All very well to give me a room – Uncle's been pushed off on a pilgrimage to Hardwar to clear a room for me – and to bring me milk and say, 'Study, Suno, study for your exam.' What about the uproar around me? These people don't know the meaning of the word Quiet. When my mother fills buckets, sloshes the kitchen floor, fries and sizzles things in the pan, she thinks she is being Quiet. The children have never even heard the word, it amazes and puzzles them. On their way back from school they fling their satchels in at my door, then tear in to snatch them back before I tear them to bits. Bawl when I pull their ears, screech when mother whacks them. Stuff themselves with her fries and then smear the grease on my books.

So I raced out of my room, with my fingers in my ears, to scream till the roof fell down about their ears. But the radio suddenly went off, the door to my parents' room suddenly opened and my father appeared, bathed and shaven, stuffed and set up with the news of the world in six different languages – his white *dhoti* blazing, his white shirt crackling, his patent leather pumps glittering. He stopped in the doorway and I stopped on the balls of my feet and wavered. My fingers came out of my ears, my hair came down over my eyes. Then he looked away from me, took his watch out of his pocket and enquired, 'Is the food ready?' in a voice that came out of his nose like the whistle of a punctual train. He skated off towards his meal, I turned and slouched back to my room. On his way to work, he looked in to say,

'Remember, Suno, I expect good results from you. Study hard, Suno.' Just behind him, I saw all the rest of them standing, peering in, silently. All of them stared at me, at the exam I was to take. At the degree I was to get. Or not get. Horrifying thought. Oh study, study, study, they all breathed at me while my father's footsteps went down the stairs, crushing each underfoot in turn. I felt their eyes on me, goggling, and their breath on me, hot with earnestness. I looked back at them, into their open mouths and staring eyes.

'Study,' I said, and found I croaked. 'I know I ought to study. And how do you expect me to study – in this mad-house? You run wild, *wild*. I'm getting out,' I screamed, leaping up and grabbing my books, 'I'm going to study outside. Even the street is quieter,' I screeched and threw myself past them and down the stairs that my father had just cowed and subjugated so that they still lay quivering, and paid no attention to the howls that broke out behind me of 'Suno, Suno, listen. Your milk – your studies – your exams, Suno!'

At first I tried the tea shop at the corner. In my reading I had often come across men who wrote at café tables – letters, verse, whole novels – over a cup of coffee or a glass of absinthe. I thought it would be simple to read a chapter of history over a cup of tea. There was no crowd in the mornings, none of my friends would be there. But the proprietor would not leave me alone. Bored, picking his nose, he wandered down from behind the counter to my table by the weighing machine and tried to pass the time of day by complaining about his piles, the new waiter and the high prices. 'And sugar,' he whined. 'How can I give you anything to put in your tea with sugar at four rupees a kilo? There's rationed sugar, I know, at two rupees, but that's not enough to feed even an ant. And the way you all sugar your tea – *hai, hai,*' he sighed, worse than my mother. I didn't answer. I frowned at my book and looked stubborn. But when I got rid of him, the waiter arrived. 'Have a biscuit?' he murmured, flicking at my table and chair with his filthy duster. 'A bun? Fritters? Make you some hot fritters?' I snarled at him but he only smiled, determined to be friendly. Just a boy, really, in a pink shirt with purple circles stamped all over it – he thought he looked so smart. He was growing sideburns, he kept fingering them. 'I'm a student, too,' he said, 'sixth class, fail. My mother wanted me to go back and try again, but I didn't like the teacher – he beat me. So I came here to look for a job. Lala-*ji* had just thrown out a boy called Hari for selling lottery tickets to the clients so he took me on. I can make out a bill . . .' He would have babbled on if Lala-*ji* had not come and shoved him into the kitchen with an oath. So it went on. I didn't read more than half a chapter that whole morning. I didn't want to go home either. I walked along the street, staring at my shoes, with my shoulders slumped in the way that makes my father scream, 'What's the matter? Haven't you bones? A spine?' I kicked some rubble along the pavement, down the drain, then stopped at the iron gates of King Edward's Park.

'Exam troubles?' asked a *gram* vendor who sat outside it, in a friendly voice. Not insinuating, but low, pleasant. 'The park's full of boys like you,' he continued in that sympathetic voice. 'I see them walk up and down, up and down with their books, like mad poets. Then I'm glad I was never sent to school,' and he began to whistle, not impertinently but so cheerfully that I stopped and stared at him. He had a crippled arm that hung out of his shirt sleeve like a leg of mutton dangling on a hook. His face was scarred as though he had been dragged out of some terrible accident. But he was shuffling hot *gram* into paper cones with his one hand and whistling like a bird, whistling the tune of, 'We are the *bul-buls* of our land, our land is Paradise.' Nodding at the

23

greenery beyond the gates, he said, 'The park's a good place to study in,' and, taking his hint, I went in.

I wonder how it is I never thought of the park before. It isn't far from our house and I sometimes went there as a boy, if I managed to run away from school, to lie on a bench, eat peanuts, shy stones at the chipmunks that came for the shells, and drink from the fountain. But then it was not as exciting as playing marbles in the street or stoning rats with my school friends in the vacant lot behind the cinema. It had straight paths, beds of flapping red flowers – cannas, I think – rows of palm trees like limp flags, a dry fountain and some green benches. Old men sat on them with their legs far apart, heads drooping over the tops of sticks, mumbling through their dentures or cackling with that mad, ripping laughter that makes children think of old men as wizards and bogey-men. Bag-like women in grey and fawn *saris* or black *borkhas* screamed, just as grey and fawn and black birds do, at children falling into the fountain or racing on rickety legs after the chipmunks and pigeons. A madman or two, prancing around in paper caps and bits of rags, munching banana peels and scratching like monkeys. Corners behind hibiscus bushes stinking of piss. Iron rails with rows of beggars contentedly dozing, scratching, gambling, with their sackcloth backs to the rails. A city park.

What I hadn't noticed, or thought of, were all the students who escaped from their city flats and families like mine to come and study here. Now, walking down a path with my history book tucked under my arm, I felt like a gatecrasher at a party or a visitor to a public library trying to control a sneeze. They all seemed to belong here, to be at home here. Dressed in loose pyjamas, they strolled up and down under the palms, books open in their hands, heads lowered into them. Or they sat in twos and threes on the grass, reading aloud in turns. Or lay full length under the trees, books spread out across their faces – sleeping, or else imbibing information through the subconscious. Opening out my book, I too strolled up and down, reading to myself in a low murmur.

In the beginning, when I first started studying in the park, I couldn't concentrate on my studies. I'd keep looking up at the boy strolling in front of me, reciting poetry in a kind of thundering whisper, waving his arms about and running his bony fingers through his hair till it stood up like a thorn bush. Or at the chipmunks that fought and played and chased each other all over the park, now and then joining forces against the sparrows over a nest or a paper cone of *gram*. Or at the madman going through the rubble at the bottom of the dry fountain and coming up with a rubber shoe, a banana peel or a piece of glittering tin that he appreciated so much that he put it in his mouth and chewed it till blood ran in strings from his mouth.

It took me time to get accustomed to the ways of the park. I went there daily, for the whole day, and soon I got to know it as well as my own room at home and found I could study there, or sleep, or daydream, as I chose. Then I fell into its routine, its rhythm, and my time moved in accordance with its time. We were like a house-owner and his house, or a turtle and its shell, or a river and its bank – so close. I resented everyone else who came to the park – I thought they couldn't possibly share my feeling for it. Except, perhaps, the students.

The park was like an hotel, or an hospital, belonging to the city but with its own order and routine, enclosed by iron rails, laid out according to prescription in rows of palms, benches and paths. If I went there very early in the morning, I'd come upon a yoga class. It consisted of young body-builders rippling their muscles like snakes as well as old crack-pots determined to keep up with the youngest and fittest, all sitting cross-legged on the grass and displaying

25

hus-mukh to the sun just rising over the palms: the Laughing Face pose it was called, but they looked like gargoyles with their mouths torn open and their thick, discoloured tongues sticking out. If I were the sun, I'd feel so disgusted by such a reception I'd just turn around and go back. And that was the simplest of their poses – after that they'd go into contortions that would embarrass an ape. Once their leader, a black and hirsute man like an aborigine, saw me watching and called me to join them. I shook my head and ducked behind an oleander. You won't catch me making an ass of myself in public. And I despise all that body-beautiful worship anyway. What's the body compared to the soul, the mind?

I'd stroll under the palms, breathing in the cool of the early morning, feeling it drive out, or wash clean, the stifling dark of the night, and try to avoid bumping into all the other early morning visitors to the park – mostly aged men sent by their wives to fetch the milk from the Government dairy booth just outside the gates. Their bottles clinking in green cloth bags and newspapers rolled up and tucked under their arms, they strutted along like stiff puppets and mostly they would be discussing philosophy. 'Ah but in Vedanta it is a different matter,' one would say, his eyes gleaming fanatically, and another would announce, 'The sage Shanakaracharya showed the way,' and some would refer to the Upanishads or the Bhagavad Puranas, but in such argumentative, hacking tones that you could see they were quite capable of coming to blows over some theological argument. Certainly it was the mind above the body for these old coots but I found nothing to admire in them either. I particularly resented it when one of them disengaged himself from the discussion long enough to notice me and throw me a gentle look of commiseration. As if he'd been through exams, too, long long ago, and knew all about them. So what?

Worst of all were the athletes, wrestlers, Mr Indias and

others who lay on their backs and were massaged with oil till every muscle shone and glittered. The men who massaged them huffed and puffed and cursed as they climbed up and down the supine bodies, pounding and pummelling the men who lay there wearing nothing but little greasy clouts, groaning and panting in a way I found obscene and disgusting. They never looked up at me or at anyone. They lived in a meaty, sweating world of their own – massages, oils, the body, a match to be fought and won – I kicked up dust in their direction but never went too close.

The afternoons would be quiet, almost empty. I would sit under a tree and read, stroll and study, doze too. Then, in the evening, as the sky softened from its blank white glare and took on shades of pink and orange and the palm trees rustled a little in an invisible breeze, the crowds would begin to pour out of Darya Ganj, Mori Gate, Chandni Chowk and the Jama Masjid bazaars and slums. Large families would come to sit about on the grass, eating peanuts and listening to a transistor radio placed in the centre of the circle. Mothers would sit together in flocks like screeching birds while children jumped into the dry fountains, broke flowers and terrorized each other. There would be a few young men moaning at the corners, waiting for a girl to roll her hips and dart her fish eyes in their direction, and then start the exciting adventure of pursuit. The children's cries would grow more piercing with the dark; frightened, shrill and exalted with mystery and farewell. I would wander back to the flat.

The exams drew nearer. Not three, not two, but only one month to go. I had to stop daydreaming and set myself tasks for every day and remind myself constantly to complete them. It grew so hot I had to give up strolling on the paths and staked out a private place for myself under a tree. I noticed the tension tightening the eyes and mouths of other

27

students – they applied themselves more diligently to their books, talked less, slept less. Everyone looked a little demented from lack of sleep. Our books seemed attached to our hands as though by roots, they were a part of us, they lived because we fed them. They were parasites and, like parasites, were sucking us dry. We mumbled to ourselves, not always consciously. Chipmunks jumped over our feet, mocking us. The *gram* seller down at the gate whistled softly 'I'm glad I never went to school, I am a *bul-bul*, I live in Paradise . . .'

My brains began to jam up. I could feel it happening, slowly. As if the oil were all used up. As if everything was getting locked together, rusted. The white cells, the grey matter, the springs and nuts and bolts. I yelled at my mother – I think it was my mother – 'What do you think I am? What do you want of me?' and crushed a glass of milk between my hands. It was sticky. She had put sugar in my milk. As if I were a baby. I wanted to cry. They wouldn't let me sleep, they wanted to see my light on all night, they made sure I never stopped studying. Then they brought me milk and sugar and made clicking sounds with their tongues. I raced out to the park. I think I sobbed as I paced up and down, up and down, in the corner that stank of piss. My head ached worse than ever. I slept all day under the tree and had to work all night.

My father laid his hand on my shoulder. I knew I was not to fling it off. So I sat still, slouching, ready to spring aside if he lifted it only slightly. 'You must get a first, Suno,' he said through his nose, 'must get a first, or else you won't get a job. Must get a job, Suno,' he sighed and wiped his nose and went off, his patent leather pumps squealing like mice. I flung myself back in my chair and howled. Get a first, get a first, get a first – like a railway engine, it went charging over me, grinding me down, and left me dead and mangled on the tracks.

28

Everything hung still and yellow in the park. I lay sluggishly on a heap of waste paper under my tree and read without seeing, slept without sleeping. Sometimes I went to the water tap that leaked and drank the leak. It tasted of brass. I spat out a mouthful. It nearly went over the feet of the student waiting for his turn at that dripping tap. I stepped aside for him. He swilled the water around his mouth and spat, too, carefully missing my feet. Wiping his mouth, he asked, 'B.A?'

'No, Inter.'

'Hu,' he burped. 'Wait till you do your B.A. Then you'll get to know.' His face was like a grey bone. It was not unkind, it simply had no expression. 'Another two weeks,' he sighed and slouched off to his own lair.

I touched my face. I thought it would be all bone, like his. I was surprised to find a bit of skin still covering it. I felt as if we were all dying in the park, that when we entered the examination hall it would be to be declared officially dead. That's what the degree was about. What else was it all about? Why were we creeping around here, hiding from the city, from teachers and parents, pretending to study and prepare? Prepare for what? We hadn't been told. Inter, they said, or B.A, or M.A. These were like official stamps – they would declare us dead. Ready for a dead world. A world in which ghosts went about, squeaking or whining, rattling or rustling. Slowly, slowly we were killing ourselves in order to join them. The ball-point pen in my pocket was the only thing that still lived, that still worked. I didn't work myself any more – I mean physically, my body no longer functioned. I was constipated, I was dying. I was lying under a yellow tree, feeling the dust sift through the leaves to cover me. It was filling my eyes, my throat. I could barely walk. I never strolled. Only on the way out of the park, late in the evening, I crept down the path under the palms, past the benches.

29

Then I saw the scene that stopped it all, stopped me just before I died.

Hidden behind an oleander was a bench. A woman lay on it, stretched out. She was a Muslim, wrapped in a black *borkha*. I hesitated when I saw this straight, still figure in black on the bench. Just then she lifted a pale, thin hand and lifted her veil. I saw her face. It lay bared, in the black folds of her *borkha*, like a flower, wax-white and composed, like a Persian lily or a tobacco flower at night. She was young. Very young, very pale, beautiful with a beauty I had never come across even in a dream. It caught me and held me tight, tight till I couldn't breathe and couldn't move. She was so white, so still, I saw she was very ill – with anaemia, perhaps, or t.b. Too pale, too white – I could see she was dying. Her head – so still and white it might have been carved if it weren't for this softness, this softness of a flower at night – lay in the lap of a very old man. Very much older than her. With spectacles and a long grey beard like a goat's, or a scholar's. He was looking down at her and caressing her face – so tenderly, so tenderly, I had never seen a hand move so gently and tenderly. Beside them, on the ground, two little girls were playing. Round little girls, rather dirty, drawing lines in the gravel. They stared at me but the man and the woman did not notice me. They never looked at anyone else, only at each other, with an expression that halted me. It was tender, loving, yes, but in an inhuman way, so intense. Divine, I felt, or insane. I stood, half-hidden by the bush, holding my book, and wondered at them. She was ill, I could see, dying. Perhaps she had only a short time to live. Why didn't he take her to the Victoria Zenana Hospital, so close to the park? Who was this man – her husband, her father, a lover? I couldn't make out although I watched them without moving, without breathing. I felt not as if I were staring rudely at strangers, but as if I were gazing at a painting or a sculpture, some work of art. Or seeing a vision. They were still and I stood still and the children stared. Then she lifted her arms above her head and laughed. Very quietly.

I broke away and hurried down the path, in order to leave them alone, in privacy. They weren't a work of art, or a vision, but real, human and alive as no one else in my life had been real and alive. I had only that glimpse of them. But I felt I could never open my books and study or take degrees after that. They belonged to the dead, and now I had seen what being alive meant. The vision burnt the surfaces of my eyes so that they watered as I groped my way up the stairs to the flat. I could hardly find my way to the bed.

It was not just the examination but everything else had suddenly withered and died, gone lifeless and purposeless when compared with this vision. My studies, my family, my life – they all belonged to the dead and only what I had seen in the park had any meaning.

Since I did not know how to span the distance between that beautiful ideal and my stupid, dull existence, I simply lay still and shut my eyes. I kept them shut so as not to see all the puzzled, pleading, indignant faces of my family around me, but I could not shut out their voices.

'Suno, Suno,' I heard them croon and coax and mourn.

'Suno, drink milk.'

'Suno, study.'

'Suno, take the exam.'

And when they tired of being so patient with me and I still would not get up, they began to crackle and spit and storm.

'Get up, Suno.'

'Study, Suno.'

'At once, Suno.'

Only my mother became resigned and gentle. She must have seen something quite out of the ordinary on my face to make her so. I felt her hand on my forehead and heard her say, 'Leave him alone. Let him sleep tonight. He is tired out, that is what it is – he has driven himself too much and now he must sleep.'

Then I heard all of them leave the room. Her hand stayed on my forehead, wet and smelling of onions, and after a bit my tears began to flow from under my lids.

'Poor Suno, sleep,' she murmured.

I went back to the park of course. But now I was changed. I had stopped being a student – I was a 'professional'. My life was dictated by the rules and routine of the park. I still had my book open on the palms of my hands as I strolled but now my eyes strayed without guilt, darting at the young girls walking in pairs, their arms linked, giggling and bumping into each other. Sometimes I stopped to rest on a bench and conversed with one of the old men, told him who my father was and what examination I was preparing for, and allowing him to tell me about his youth, his politics, his philosophy, his youth and again his youth. Or I joked with the other students, sitting on the grass and throwing peanut shells at the chipmunks, and shocking them, I could see, with my irreverence and cynicism about the school, the exam, the system. Once I even nodded at the yoga teacher and exchanged a few words with him. He suggested I join his class and I nodded vaguely and said I would think it over. It might help. My father says I need help. He says I am hopeless but that I need help. I just laugh but I know that he knows I will never appear for the examination, I will never come up to that hurdle or cross it – life has taken a different path for me, in the form of a search, not a race as it is for him, for them.

Yes, it is a search, a kind of perpetual search for me and now that I have accepted it and don't struggle, I find it satisfies me entirely, and I wander about the park as freely as a prince in his palace garden. I look over the benches, I glance behind the bushes, and wonder if I shall ever get another glimpse of that strange vision that set me free. I never have but I keep hoping, wishing.

❧ Surface Textures ❧

It was all her own fault, she later knew – but how could she have helped it? When she stood, puckering her lips, before the fruit barrow in the market and, after sullen consideration, at last plucked a rather small but nicely ripened melon out of a heap on display, her only thought had been Is it worth a *rupee* and fifty *paise*? The lichees looked more poetic, in large clusters like some prickly grapes of a charming rose colour, their long stalks and stiff grey leaves tied in a bunch above them – but were expensive. Mangoes were what the children were eagerly waiting for – the boys, she knew, were raiding the mango trees in the school compound daily and their stomach-aches were a result, she told them, of the unripe mangoes they ate and for which they carried paper packets of salt to school in their pockets instead of handkerchiefs – but, leave alone the expense, the ones the fruiterer held up to her enticingly were bound to be sharp and sour for all their parakeet shades of rose and saffron; it was still too early for mangoes. So she put the melon in her string bag, rather angrily – paid the man his one *rupee* and fifty *paise* which altered his expression from one of promise and enticement to that of disappointment and contempt, and trailed off towards the vegetable barrow.

That, she later saw, was the beginning of it all, for if the melon seemed puny to her and boring to the children, from the start her husband regarded it with eyes that seemed newly opened. One would have thought he had never seen a melon before. All through the meal his eyes remained fixed on the plate in the centre of the table with its big button of a yellow melon. He left most of his rice and pulses on his plate, to her indignation. While she scolded, he reached out to touch the melon that so captivated him. With one finger he stroked the coarse grain of its rind, rough with the upraised criss-cross of pale veins. Then he ran his fingers up and down the green streaks that divided it into even quarters as by green silk threads, so tenderly. She was clearing away the plates and did not notice till she came back from the kitchen.

'Aren't you going to cut it for us?' she asked, pushing the knife across to him.

He gave her a reproachful look as he picked up the knife and went about dividing the melon into quarter-moon portions with sighs that showed how it pained him.

'Come on, come on,' she said, roughly, 'the boys have to get back to school.'

He handed them their portions and watched them scoop out the icy orange flesh with a fearful expression on his face – as though he were observing cannibals at a feast. She had not the time to pay any attention to it then but later described it as horror. And he did not eat his own slice. When the boys rushed away, he bowed his head over his plate and regarded it.

'Are you going to fall asleep?' she cried, a little frightened.

'Oh no,' he said, in that low mumble that always exasperated her – it seemed a sign to her of evasiveness and pusillanimity, this mumble – 'Oh no, no.' Yet he did not object when she seized the plate and carried it off to the kitchen, merely picked up the knife that was left behind and, picking a flat melon seed off its edge where it had remained stuck, he held it between two fingers, fondling it delicately. Continuing to do this, he left the house.

The melon might have been the apple of knowledge for Harish – so deadly its poison that he did not even need to bite into it to imbibe it: that long, devoted look had been enough. As he walked back to his office which issued ration cards to the population of their town, he looked about him vaguely but with hunger, his eyes resting not on the things on which people's eyes normally rest – signboards, the traffic, the number of an approaching bus – but on such things, normally considered nondescript and unimportant, as the paving stones on which their feet momentarily pressed, the length of wire in a railing at the side of the road, a pattern of grime on the windowpane of a disused printing press . . . Amongst such things his eyes roved and hunted and, when he was seated at his desk in the office, his eyes continued to slide about – that was Sheila's phrase later: 'slide about' – in a musing, calculating way, over the surface of the crowded desk, about the corners of the room, even across the ceiling. He seemed unable to focus them on a file or a card long enough to put to them his signature – they lay unsigned and the people in the queue outside went for another day without rice and sugar and kerosene for their lamps and Janta cookers. Harish searched – slid about, hunted, gazed – and at last found sufficiently interesting a thick book of rules that lay beneath a stack of files. Then his hand reached out – not to pull the book to him or open it, but to run the ball of his thumb across the edge of the pages. In their large number and irregular cut, so closely laid out like some crisp palimpsest, his eyes seemed to find something of riveting interest and his thumb of tactile wonder. All afternoon he massaged the cut edges of the book's seven hundred odd pages – tenderly, wonderingly. All afternoon his eyes gazed upon them with strange devotion. At five o'clock, punctually, the office shut and the queue disintegrated into vociferous grumbles and threats as people went home instead of to the ration shops, empty-handed instead of loaded with those necessary but, to Harish, so dull comestibles.

Although Government service is as hard to depart from as to enter – so many letters to be written, forms to be filled, files to be circulated, petitions to be made that it hardly seems worthwhile – Harrish was, after some time, dismissed – time he happily spent judging the difference between white blotting paper and pink (pink is flatter, denser, white spongier) and the texture of blotting paper stained with ink and that which is fresh, that which has been put to melt in a saucer of cold tea and that which has been doused in a pot of ink. Harish was dismissed.

The first few days Sheila stormed and screamed like some shrill, wet hurricane about the house. 'How am I to go to market and buy vegetables for dinner? I don't even have enough for that. What am I to feed the boys tonight? No more milk for them. The washerwoman is asking for her bill to be paid. Do you hear? Do you *hear*? And we shall have to leave this flat. Where shall we go?' He listened – or didn't – sitting on a cushion before her mirror, fingering the small silver box in which she kept the red *kum-kum* that daily cut a gash from one end of her scalp to the other after her toilet. It was of dark, almost blackened silver, with a whole forest embossed on it – banana groves, elephants, peacocks and jackals. He rubbed his thumb over its cold, raised surface.

After that, she wept. She lay on her bed in a bath of tears and perspiration, and it was only because of the kindness of their neighbours that they did not starve to death the very first week, for even those who most disliked and distrusted Harish – 'Always said he looks like a hungry hyena,' said Mr Bhatia who lived below their flat, 'not human at all, but like a hungry, hunchbacked hyena hunting along the road' –

felt for the distraught wife and the hungry children (who did not really mind as long as there were sour green mangoes to steal and devour) and looked to them. Such delicacies as Harish's family had never known before arrived in stainless steel and brass dishes, with delicate unobtrusiveness. For a while wife and children gorged on sweetmeats made with fresh buffalo milk, on pulses cooked according to grandmother's recipes, on stuffed bread and the first pomegranates of the season. But, although delicious, these offerings came in small quantities and irregularly and soon they were really starving.

'I suppose you want me to take the boys home to my parents,' said Sheila bitterly, getting up from the bed. 'Any other man would regard that as the worst disgrace of all – but not you. What is my shame to you? I will have to hang my head and crawl home and beg my father to look after us since you won't,' and that was what she did. He was sorry, very sorry to see her pack the little silver *kum-kum* box in her black trunk and carry it away.

Soon after, officials of the Ministry of Works, Housing and Land Development came and turned Harish out, cleaned and painted the flat and let in the new tenants who could hardly believe their luck – they had been told so often they couldn't expect a flat in that locality for at least another two years.

The neighbours lost sight of Harish. Once some children reported they had seen him lying under the *pipal* tree at the corner of their school compound, staring fixedly at the red gashes cut into the papery bark and, later, a boy who commuted to school on a suburban train claimed to have seen him on the railway platform, sitting against a railing like some tattered beggar, staring across the criss-cross of shining rails. But next day, when the boy got off the train, he did not see Harish again.

Harish had gone hunting. His slow, silent walk gave him

the appearance of sliding rather than walking over the surface of the roads and fields, rather like a snail except that his movement was not as smooth as a snail's but stumbling as if he had only recently become one and was still unused to the pace. Not only his eyes and his hands but even his bare feet seemed to be feeling the earth carefully, in search of an interesting surface. Once he found it, he would pause, his whole body would gently collapse across it and hours – perhaps days – would be devoted to its investigation and worship. Outside the town the land was rocky and bare and this was Harish's especial paradise, each rock having a surface of such exquisite roughness, of such perfection in shape and design, as to keep him occupied and ecstatic for weeks together. Then the river beyond the rock quarries drew him away and there he discovered the joy of fingering silk-smooth stalks and reeds, stems and leaves.

Shepherd children, seeing him stumble about the reeds, plunging thigh-deep into the water in order to pull out a water lily with its cool, sinuous stem, fled screaming, not certain whether this was a man or a hairy water snake. Their mothers came, some with stones and some with canes at the ready, but when they saw Harish, his skin parched to a violet shade, sitting on the bank and gazing at the transparent stem of the lotus, they fell back, crying, 'Wah!' gathered closer together, advanced, dropped their canes and stones, held their children still by their hair and shoulders, and came to bow to him. Then they hurried back to the village, chattering. They had never had a Swami to themselves, in these arid parts. Nor had they seen a Swami who looked holier, more inhuman than Harish with his matted hair, his blue, starved skin and single-focused eyes. So, in the evening, one brought him a brass vessel of milk, another a little rice. They pushed their children before them and made them drop flowers at his feet. When Harish stooped and felt among the offerings for something his fingers could

39

respond to, they were pleased, they felt accepted. 'Swami-ji,' they whispered, 'speak.'

Harish did not speak and his silence made him still holier, safer. So they worshipped him, fed and watched over him, interpreting his moves in their own fashion, and Harish, in turn, watched over their offerings and worshipped.

~ Sale ~

There they are, at the door now, banging. They had met
him, written a note and made an appointment – and here
they are, as a direct result of it all, rattling. He stands on the
other side of the door, in the dusk-mottled room, fingering
an unshaven chin and dropping cigarette butts on the floor
which is already littered with them. There is a pause in the
knocking. He hears their voices – querulous, impatient. He
turns and silently goes towards the inner door that opens
onto a passage. He pushes it ajar, quietly, holding his breath.
At the end of the passage another door stands open: it is like
a window or an alcove illuminated by the deep glow of the
fire. There his wife sits, kneading dough in a brass bowl,
with her head bowed so that her long hair broods down to
her shoulders on either side of her heavy, troubled face. The
red border of her sari cuts a bright gash through the still
tableau. The child sits on the mat beside her, silent,
absorbed in the mysteries of a long-handled spoon which he
turns over with soft, wavering fingers that are unaccustomed to the unsympathetic steel. His head, too, is
bowed so that his father, behind him, can see the small
wisps of hair on the back of his neck. He looks at them,
holding his breath till it begins to hurt his chest. Then the

knocking is resumed and his wife, hearing it, raises her head. She sees him then, at the door, like a dog hanging about, wanting something, and immediately her nostrils flare. 'Can't you answer the door?' she cries. 'What's the matter with you? It must be them – this is your chance.' Startled, the child drops the spoon with a clatter. Quickly he shuts the door. Then he goes and opens the front door and lets them in.

'We were about to give up,' one man cries, laughing, and brings in his friend and also a woman, seeing whom the artist, who is not expecting her, finds himself dismayed and confused. A woman – therefore someone in league with his wife, he thinks, and stares at her lush, unreluctant face and the bright enamelled ear-rings that frame it. He is silent. The two men stare at him.

'You *were* expecting us, weren't you?' enquires the jovial man whom he had liked, once. 'We wrote—'

'Yes,' he murmurs. 'Oh yes, yes,' and stands there, on the threshold, with an empty match box in his hand, his face looking like a house from which ghosts had driven away all inhabitants.

Then the man introduces his wife. 'She also paints,' he says, 'and was so interested in seeing your pictures, I brought her along. You don't mind, do you?'

'No,' he says, gathering himself together with a laboured effort, and steps aside to let them in. Then it is they who are silent, staring in dismay at the shambles about them. There are pictures to look at, yes, but one lies on the floor with a bundle of rags and some cigarette stubs on it, another is propped up on a shelf with bottles of hair oil, clay toys and calendars before it, and others have drifted off the wooden divan into corners of the room, peering out from under old newspapers and dirty clothes. The artist watches them, wondering at the imbecility of their appearance as they huddle together and gape. 'Oh,' he says, recovering, 'the light,' and switches it on. It is unshaded and hangs low over the flat table at which he paints so that they are illuminated weirdly from the waist downwards, leaving their faces more confused with shadows than before. The woman is quickest to relax, to make herself known, to become acquainted. 'Ah,' she cries, hurrying to the shelf to pull out a picture. 'What are they?' she asks him, gazing first at the flowers that blaze across the dirty paper, then at him, coaxing him for their secret with an avidly enquiring look. 'Not cannas, not lotuses – what can they be?'

He smiles at her curiosity. 'Nothing,' he says. 'Not real flowers – just anything at all.'

'Really!' she exclaims, shaking her enamelled ear-rings. 'How wonderful to be able to imagine such forms, such colours. Look, Ram, aren't they pretty?' The two men become infected by her exaggerated attitude of relaxation. They begin to prowl about the room, now showing amusement at the litter which is, after all, only to be expected in an artist's studio, then crinkling their noses for, one has to admit, it *does* smell, and then showing surprised interest in the pictures of which they have come to select one for their home which is newly built and now to be furnished. What with the enthusiasm and thoroughness they bring to their task, the rags and grime of the studio are soon almost obliterated by the fanfare of colour that spills forth, a crazy whorl of them, unknown colours that cannot be named, spilling out of forms that cannot be identified. One cannot pinpoint any school, any technique, any style – one can only admit oneself in the presence of a continuous and inspired act of creation: so they tell themselves. The woman gives cry upon cry of excitement and turns again and again to the artist who stands watching them thoughtfully. 'But how did you get this colour? You must tell me because I paint – and I could never get anything like this. What is it?'

43

'Ahh, Naples Yellow,' he says, as if making a guess.

'No, but there is some orange in it too.'

'Ah yes, a little orange also.'

'And green?'

'Yes, a little perhaps.'

'No, but that special tinge – how did you get it? A little bit of white – or flesh pink? What is it? Ram, Ram, just look, isn't it pretty – this weird bird? I don't suppose it has a name?'

'No, no, it is not real. I am a city man, I know nothing about birds.'

'But you know everything about birds! And flowers. I suppose they *are* birds and flowers, all these marvellous things. And your paintings are full of them. How can it possibly be that you have never seen them?'

He has to laugh then – she is so artless, so completely without any vestige of imagination, and so completely unlike his wife. 'Look,' he says, suddenly buoyant, and points to the window. She has to stand on her toes to look out of the small aperture, through the bars, and then she gazes out with all the intentness she feels he expects of her, at the deep, smoke-ridden twilight wound around the ill-lit slum, the smoking heaps of dung-fires and the dark figures that sit and stand in it hopelessly. Like fog-horns, conch shells begin to blow as tired housewives summon up their flagging spirits for the always lovely, always comforting ritual of evening prayers. She tries to pierce the scene with her sharp eyes, trying to see what he sees in it, till she hears him laughing behind her with a cracked kind of hilarity. 'There you see – my birds and my flowers,' he tells her, clapping his hands as though enjoying a practical joke he has played on her. 'I see a tram – and that is my mountain. I see a letter-box – and that is my tree. Listen! Do you hear my birds?' He raises his hand and, with its gesture, ushers in the evening voices of children uttering those cries and calls

44

peculiar to the time of parting, the time of relinquishing their games, before they enter their homes and disappear into sleep – voices filled with an ecstasy of knowledge, of sensation drawn to an apex, brought on by the realization of imminent departure and farewell: voices panicky with love, with lament, with fear and sacrifice.

The artist watches the three visitors and finds them attentive, puzzled. 'There,' he says, dropping his hand. 'There are my birds. I don't see them – but I hear them and imagine how they look. It is easy, no, when you can hear them so clearly?'

'You are a magician,' says the quiet man, shaking his head and turning to a crayon drawing of pale birds delicately stalking the shallows of a brooding sea. 'Look at these – I can't believe you haven't actually painted them on the spot.'

'No, I have not, but I do know the sea. You know, I am a fisherman! I should have been – my people are. How do you like this one of fishing boats? I used to see them coming in like this, in the evening, with the catch. And then my mother would cook one large one for dinner – oh, it was good, good!'

They all stand around him, smiling at this unexpected burst of childish exuberance. 'You paint from memory then?' enquires one, but the woman cries 'You like fish? You must come and eat it at our house one day – I cook fish very well.'

'I will, I will,' he cries, scurrying about as though he were looking for something he had suddenly remembered he needed, hunting out seascapes for them to see, and more of the successful flowers. 'Oh, I will love that – to see this new house of yours and eat a meal cooked by you. Yes, I will come. Here, look, another one – a canal scene. Do you like it? That is paddy growing there – it is so green . . .' Now he wants to turn out the entire studio for them, bring out his best. He chatters, they laugh. Pictures fall to the floor.

45

Crayons are smeared, oils are smudged – but he does not mind. He does not even sign his pictures. When the woman pauses over a pastel that is blurred by some stroke of carelessness, he says 'Oh that is nothing, I can touch it up. Do you see the blue? Do you like it? Yes, I will see your paintings and I will tell you plainly what I like and what I don't like, and you will appreciate anyway. Oh, I love fish . . .' Only now and then he grows aware of his wife, breathing heavily because of the weight of the child asleep on her arm, straining to hear at the door, frowning because she cannot understand, is not certain, is worried, worried to death . . . and then he draws down the corners of his mouth and is silent. But when a picture of curled flowers is brought to him, he stares at it till it comes into proper focus and explains it to them. 'Ah,' he says, 'I painted that long ago – for my son, when he was born. I wanted him to have flowers, flowers all about his bed, under his head, at his feet, everywhere. And I did not have any. I did not know of a garden from where I could get some. So I painted them. That is one of them. Ah yes, yes,' he smiles, and the three who watch him grow tender, sympathetic. The woman says, '*This* one? It is your son's? How lovely – how lucky.'

'No,' he cries loudly. 'I mean, you can have it. Do you like it? It is what you want for your new house?'

'Oh no,' she says softly and puts it away. 'You painted it for your child. I can't take it from him.'

The artist finds himself sweating and exhausted – he had not realized how he was straining himself. He has had nothing but tea and cigarettes since early that morning and there is no breath of air coming through the barred window. He wipes his face with his hand and blotches another crayon with his wet fingers as he picks it up and flings it away. 'Then what do you want?' he asks in a flat voice. 'What do you like? What do you want to have – a flower picture or a landscape?'

'Perhaps figures – people always make a room seem bright.'

'I don't paint figures,' he says shortly. 'You told me you wanted a landscape. Here they are – all sizes, big, small, medium; hills, seas, rivers; green, blue, yellow. Is there nothing you like?'

'Yes, yes,' they all assure him together, upset by his change of tone, and one holds up a picture at arm's length to admire it lavishly, another bends to shuffle through the pile on the table. But there are so many, they say, it is hard to choose. That is nothing, he says, *he* will choose for them. Oh no, they laugh, glancing to see if he is serious, for they have something very special in mind – something that will light up their whole house, become its focal point, radiate and give their home a tone, an atmosphere. No, not this one, not *quite* – it is lovely, but . . . Before he knows it, they are at the door, descending the stairs with one backward look at all the heroic mass of colour inside, saying goodbye. He rushes down the stairs after them, spreading out his arms. Their car stands under the lamp-post. He flings himself at the door, hangs on to it.

'There is not one you liked? I thought you had come to buy – you said—'

'Yes, we wanted to,' says the man whom he had liked, once. 'But not one of these. You see, we have something very special in mind, something quite extraordinary—'

'But – not one of those I showed you? I thought you liked them – you said—'

'I did, I did,' chirps the woman from the soft recesses of the back seat. 'Oh and those lovely flowers you painted for your son – *lucky* child!'

'You liked them? I will paint you another like it, just like it—'

'But we wanted a landscape really,' says the man. 'Some-

thing in those cool greys and whites. Perhaps a snow scene –
now *that* would be something different.'

'Snow?' shouts the artist. 'I will paint snow. I will paint
the Himalayas for you. How big do you want it? So big?
So?'

'No, no,' they laugh. 'Not so big. That would be too
expensive.'

'All right, smaller. I will paint it. By the end of the week
you will have it.'

They laugh at his haste, his trembling, shrill excitement.
'But, my friend, have you ever seen snow?' enquires the
jovial one, patting his arm.

'Ah!' he gives such a cry that it halts them in their movements of departure, to turn and see him spread out his arms
till his fingers reach out of the smoke of the dung fires and
the dust of the unlit lanes, to reach out to the balm of ice and
snow and isolation. 'I will paint such snow for you as you
have never seen, as no one has ever painted. I can see it all,
here,' and he taps his forehead with such emphasis that they
smile – he is quite a comic. Or even a bit crazy. Drunk?

'Now, now, my friend,' says the man, patting his arm
again. 'Don't be in a hurry about it. You paint it when you
are in the mood. Then it will be good.'

'I am in the mood now,' he cries. 'I am always in the
mood, don't you see? Tomorrow, tomorrow I will have it
ready. I will bring it to your house. Give me the address!'

They laugh. The engine stutters to life and there is a
metallic finality in the sound of the doors being shut. But he
clings to the handle, thrusts his head in, his eyes blazing.
'And will you give me an advance?' he asks tensely. 'I need
money, my friend. Can you give me an advance?'

The woman creeps away into a corner, wrapping herself
closely in a white shawl. One man, in embarrassment, falls
silent. The other laughs and puts his hands in his pockets,
then draws them out to show they are empty. 'Brother, if I

48

had some with me, I would give it to you – all of it – but since we only came to see, I didn't bring any. I'm sorry.'

'I need it.'

'Listen, when you bring the picture, I will give you something, even if I don't want it, I will give you something – in advance, for the one we will buy. But today, just now, I have nothing.'

The artist steps back to let them go. As they drive out of the lane and the smoke smudges and obscures the tail-lights, he hears his wife come out on the stairs behind him.

﹌ Pineapple Cake ﹌

Victor was a nervous rather than rebellious child. But it made no difference to his mother: she had the same way of dealing with nerves and rebels.

'You like pineapple cake, don't you? Well, come along, get dressed quickly – yes, yes, the velvet shorts – the new shoes, yes – hurry – pineapple cake for good boys. . . .'

So it had gone all afternoon and, by holding out the bait of pineapple cake, his favourite, Mrs Fernandez had the boy dressed in his new frilled shirt and purple velvet shorts and new shoes that bit his toes and had him sitting quietly in church right through the long ceremony. Or so she thought, her faith in pineapple cake being matched only by her faith in Our Lady of Mount Mary, Bandra Hill, Bombay. Looking at Victor, trying hard to keep his loud breathing bottled inside his chest and leaning down to see what made his shoes so vicious, you might have thought she had been successful, but success never satisfies and Mrs Fernandez sighed to think how much easier it would have been if she had had a daughter instead. Little girls love weddings, little girls play at weddings, little girls can be dressed in can-can petticoats and frocks like crêpe-paper bells of pink and orange, their oiled and ringleted hair crowned with rustling wreaths of paper flowers. She glanced around her rather tiredly to hear the church rustling and crepitating with excited little girls, dim and dusty as it was, lit here and there by a blazing afternoon window of red and blue glass, a flare of candles or a silver bell breathless in the turgid air. This reminded her how she had come to this church to pray and light candles to Our Lady when she was expecting Victor, and it made her glance down at him and wonder why he was perspiring so. Yes, the collar of the frilled shirt was a bit tight and the church was airless and stuffy but it wasn't very refined of him to sweat so. Of course all the little boys in her row seemed to be in the same state – each one threatened or bribed into docility, their silence straining in their chests, soundlessly clamouring. Their eyes were the eyes of prisoners, dark and blazing at the ignominy and boredom and injustice of it all. When they shut their eyes and bowed their heads in prayer, it was as if half the candles in church had gone out, and it was darker.

Relenting, Mrs Fernandez whispered, under cover of the sonorous prayer led by the grey padre in faded purple, 'Nearly over now, Victor. In a little while we'll be going to tea – pineapple cake for you.'

Victor hadn't much faith in his mother's promises. They had a way of getting postponed or cancelled on account of some small accidental lapse on his part. He might tear a hole in his sleeve – no pocket money. Or stare a minute too long at Uncle Arthur who was down on a visit from Goa and had a wen on the back of his bald head – no caramel custard for pudding. So he would not exchange looks with her but stared stolidly down at his polished shoes, licked his dry lips and wondered if there would be Fanta or Coca-Cola at tea.

Then the ceremony came to an end. How or why, he could not tell, sunk so far below eye-level in that lake of breathless witnesses to the marriage of Carmen Maria Braganza of Goa and George de Mello of Byculla, Bombay.

51

He had seen nothing of it, only followed, disconsolately and confusedly, the smells and sounds of it, like some underground creature, an infant mole, trying to make out what went on outside its burrow, and whether it was alarming or enticing. Now it was over and his mother was digging him in the ribs, shoving him out, hurrying him by running into his heels, and now they were streaming out with the tide. At the door he made out the purple of the padre's robes, he was handed a pink paper flower by a little girl who held a silver basket full of them and whose face gleamed with fanatic self-importance, and then he was swept down the stairs, held onto by his elbow and, once on ground level, his mother was making a din about finding a vehicle to take them to the reception at Green's. 'The tea will be at Green's, you know,' she had been saying several times a day for weeks now. 'Those de Mellos must have money – they can't be so badly off – tea at Green's, after all.'

It was no easy matter, she found, to be taken care of, for although there was a whole line of cabs at the kerb, they all belonged to the more important members of the de Mello and Braganza families. When Mrs Fernandez realized this, she set her lips together and looked dangerously wrathful, and the party atmosphere began quickly to dissolve in the acid of bad temper and the threat to her dignity. Victor stupidly began a fantasy of slipping out of her hold and breaking into a toy shop for skates and speeding ahead of the whole caravan on a magic pair, to arrive at Green's before the bride, losing his mother on the way . . . But she found two seats, in the nick of time, in a taxi that already contained a short, broad woman in a purple net frock and a long thin man with an adam's apple that struggled to rise above his polka-dotted bow tie and then slipped down again with an audible croak. The four of them sat squeezed together and the women made little remarks about how beautiful Carmen Maria had looked and how the de Mellos couldn't be badly off, tea at Green's, after all. 'Green's', the woman in the purple net frock yelled into the taxi driver's ear and gave her bottom an important shake that knocked Victor against the door. He felt that he was being shoved out, he was not wanted, he had no place here. This must have made him look peaked for his mother squeezed his hand and whispered, 'You've been a good boy – pineapple cake for you.' Victor sat still, not breathing. The man with the adam's apple stretched his neck longer and longer, swivelled his head about on the top of it and said nothing, but the frog in his throat gurgled to itself.

Let out of the taxi, Victor looked about him at the wonders of Bombay harbour while the elders tried to be polite and yet not pay the taxi. Had his father brought him here on a Sunday outing, with a ferry boat ride and a fresh coconut drink for treats, he would have enjoyed the Arab dhows with their muddy sails, the ships and tankers and seagulls and the Gateway of India like a coloured version of the photograph in his history book, but it was too unexpected. He had been promised pineapple cake at Green's, sufficiently overwhelming in itself – he hadn't the wherewithal to cope with the Gateway of India as well.

Instinctively he put out his hand to find his mother's and received another shock – she had slipped on a pair of gloves, dreadfully new ones of crackling nylon lace, like fresh bandages on her purple hands. She squeezed his hand, saying 'If you want to do soo-soo, tell me, I'll find the toilet. Don't you go and wet your pants, man.' Horrified, he pulled away but she caught him by the collar and led him into the hotel and up the stairs to the tea room where refreshments were to be served in celebration of Carmen Maria's and George de Mello's wedding. The band was still playing 'Here Comes The Bride' when Victor and his mother entered.

Here there was a repetition of the scene over the taxi: this

53

time it was seats at a suitable table that Mrs Fernandez demanded, could not find, then spotted, was turned away from and, finally, led to two others by a slippery-smooth waiter used to such scenes. The tables had been arranged in the form of the letter E, and covered with white cloths. Little vases marched up the centres of the tables, sprouting stiff zinnias and limp periwinkles. The guests, chief and otherwise, seemed flustered by the arrangements, rustled about, making adjustments and readjustments, but the staff showed no such hesitations over protocol. They seated the party masterfully, had the tables laid out impeccably and, when the band swung into the 'Do Re Mi' song from *The Sound of Music*, brought in the wedding cake. Everyone craned to see Carmen Maria cut it, and Victor's mother gave him a pinch that made him half-rise from his chair, whispering, 'Stand up if you can't see, man, stand up to see Carmen Maria cut the cake.' There was a burst of laughter, applause and raucous congratulation with an undertone of ribaldry that unnerved Victor and made him sink down on his chair, already a bit sick.

The band was playing a lively version of 'I am Sixteen, Going on Seventeen' when Victor heard a curious sound, as of a choked drain being forced. Others heard it too for suddenly chairs were being scraped back, people were standing up, some of them stepped backwards and nearly fell on top of Victor who hastily got off his chair. The mother of the bride, in her pink and silver gauzes, ran up, crying 'Oh no, oh no, no, no!'

Two seats down sat the man with the long, thin neck in which an adam's apple rose and fell so lugubriously. Only he was no longer sitting. He was sprawled over his chair, his head hanging over the back in a curiously unhinged way, as though dangling at the end of a rope. The woman in the purple net dress was leaning over him and screaming 'Aub, Aub, my darling Aubrey! Help my darling Aubrey!' Victor

54

gave a shiver and stepped back and back till someone caught and held him.

Someone ran past – perhaps one of those confident young waiters who knew all there was to know – shouting 'Phone for a doctor, quick! Call Dr Patel,' and then there was a long, ripping groan all the way down the tables which seemed to come from the woman in the purple net dress or perhaps from the bride's mother, Victor could not tell – 'Oh, why did it have to happen *today*? Couldn't he have gone into another day?' Carmen Maria, the bride, began to sob frightenedly. After that someone grasped the long-necked old man by his knees and armpits and carried him away, his head and his shoes dangling like stuffed paper bags. The knot of guests around him loosened and came apart to make way for what was obviously a corpse.

Dimly, Victor realized this. The screams and sobs of the party-dressed women underlined it. So did the slow, stunned way in which people rose from the table, scraped back their chairs and retreated to the balcony, shaking their heads and muttering, 'An omen, I tell you, it must be an omen.' Victor made a hesitant move towards the balcony – perhaps he would see the hearse arrive.

But Victor's mother was holding him by the arm and she gave it an excited tug. 'Sit *down*, man,' she whispered furtively, 'here comes the pineapple cake,' and, to his amazement, a plate of pastries was actually on the table now – iced, coloured and gay. 'Take it, take the pineapple cake,' she urged him, pushing him towards the plate, and when the boy didn't move but stared down at the pastry dish as though it were the corpse on the red rexine sofa, her mouth gave an impatient twitch and she reached out to fork the pineapple cake onto her own plate. She ate it quickly. Wiping her mouth primly, she said, 'I think we'd better go now.'

🍃 The Accompanist 🍃

It was only on the night of the concert, when we assembled
on stage behind drawn curtains, that he gave me the notes to
be played. I always hoped he would bring himself to do this
earlier and I hovered around him all evening, tuning his *sitar*
and preparing his betel leaves, but he would not speak to me
at all. There were always many others around him – his
hosts and the organizers of the concert, his friends and
well-wishers and disciples – and he spoke and laughed with
all of them, but always turned his head away when I came
near. I was not hurt: this was his way with me, I was used to
it. Only I wished he would tell me what he planned to play
before the concert began so that I could prepare myself. I
found it difficult to plunge immediately, like lightning,
without pause or preparation, into the music, as he did. But
I had to learn how to make myself do this, and did. In
everything, he led me, I followed.

For fifteen years now, this has been our way of life. It
began the day when I was fifteen years old and took a new
tanpura, made by my father who was a maker of musical
instruments and also played several of them with talent and
distinction, to a concert hall where Ustad Rahim Khan was
to play that night. He had ordered a new *tanpura* from my

father who was known to all musicians for the fine quality of the instruments he made for them, with love as well as a deep knowledge of music. When I arrived at the hall, I looked around for someone to give the *tanpura* to but the hall was in darkness as the management would not allow the musicians to use the lights before the show and only on stage was a single bulb lit, lighting up the little knot of musicians and surrounding them with elongated, restless and, somehow, ominous shadows. The Ustad was tuning his *sitar*, pausing to laugh and talk to his companions every now and then. They were all talking and no one saw me. I stood for a long time in the doorway, gazing at the famous Ustad of whom my father had spoken with such reverence. 'Do not mention the matter of payment,' he had warned me. 'He is doing us an honour by ordering a *tanpura* from us.' This had impressed me and, as I gazed at him, I knew my father had been truthful about him. He was only tuning his *sitar*, casually and haphazardly, but his fingers were the fingers of a god, absolutely in control of his instrument and I knew nothing but perfection could come of such a relationship between a musician and his instrument.

So I slowly walked up the aisle, bearing the new *tanpura* in my arms and all the time gazing at the man in the centre of that restless, chattering group, himself absolutely in repose, controlled and purposeful. As I came closer to the stage, I could see his face beneath the long locks of hair, and the face, too, was that of a god: it was large, perhaps heavy about the jaws, but balanced by a wide forehead and with blazing black eyes that were widely spaced. His nostrils and his mouth, too, were large, royal, but intelligent, controlled. And as I looked into his face, telling myself of all the impressive points it contained, he looked down at me. I do not know what he saw, what he could see in the darkness and shadows of the unlit hall, but he smiled with sweet gentleness and beckoned to me. 'What do you have there?' he called.

Then I had the courage to run up the steps at the side of the stage and straight to him. I did not look at anyone else. I did not even notice the others or care for their reaction to me. I went straight to him who was the centre of the gathering, of the stage and thereafter of my entire life, and presented the *tanpura* to him.

'Ah, the new *tanpura*. From Mishra-*ji* in the music lane? You have come from Mishra-*ji*?'

'He is my father,' I whispered, kneeling before him and still looking into his face, unable to look away from it, it drew me so to him, close to him.

'Mishra-*ji*'s son?' he said, with a deep, friendly laugh. After running his fingers over the *tanpura* strings, he put it down on the carpet and suddenly stretched out his hand so that the fine white muslin sleeve of his *kurta* fell back and bared his arm, strong and muscular as an athlete's, with veins finely marked upon the taut skin, and fondled my chin. 'Do you play?' he asked. 'My *tanpura* player has not arrived. Where is he?' he called over his shoulder. 'Why isn't he here?'

All his friends and followers began to babble. Some said he was ill, in the hotel, some that he had met friends and gone with them. No one really knew. The Ustad shook his head thoughtfully, then said, 'He is probably in his cups again, the old drunkard. I won't have him play for me any more. Let the child play,' and immediately he picked up his *sitar* and began to play, bowing his head over the instrument, a kind of veil of thoughtfulness and concentration falling across his face so that I knew I could not interrupt with the questions I wished to ask. He glanced at me, once, briefly, and beckoned to me to pick up the *tanpura* and play. '*Raga Dipak*,' he said, and told me the notes to be played in such a quick undertone that I would not have heard him had

58

I not been so acutely attentive to him. And I sat down behind him, on the bare floor, picked up the new *tanpura* my father had made, and began to play the three notes he gave me – the central one, its octave and quintet – over and over again, creating the discreet background web of sound upon which he improvised and embroidered his *raga*.

And so I became the *tanpura* player for Ustad Rahim Khan's group. I have played for him since then, for no one else. I have done nothing else. It is my entire life. I am thirty years old now and my Ustad has begun to turn grey, and often he interrupts a concert with that hacking cough that troubles him, and he takes more opium than he should to quieten it – I give it to him myself for he always asks me to prepare it. We have travelled all over India and played in every city, at every season. It is his life, and mine. We share this life, this music, this following. What else can there possibly be for me in this world? Some have tried to tempt me from his side, but I have stayed with him, not wishing for anything else, anything more.

Ours is a world formed and defined and enclosed not so much by music, however, as by a human relationship on solid ground level the relationship of love. Not an abstract quality, like music, or an intellectual one, like art, but a common human quality lived on an everyday level of reality – the quality of love. So I believe. What else is it that weaves us together as we play, so that I know every movement he will make before he himself does, and he can count on me to be always where he wants me? We never diverge: we leave and we arrive together. Is this not love? No marriage was closer.

When I was a boy many other things existed on earth for me. Of course music was always important, the chief household deity of a family musical by tradition. The central hall of our house was given over to the making of musical instruments for which my father, and his father before him, were famous. From it rose sounds not only of the craft involved – the knocking, tapping, planing and tuning – but also of music. Music vibrated there constantly, sometimes harmoniously and sometimes discordantly, a quality of the very air of our house: dense, shaped by infinite variation, and never still. I was only a child, perhaps four years old, when my father began waking me at four o'clock every morning to go down to the hall with him and take lessons from him on the *tanpura*, the harmonium, the *sitar* and even the *tabla*. He could play them all and wished to see for which I had an aptitude. Music being literally the air we breathed in that tall, narrow house in the lane that had belonged for generations to the makers of musical instruments in that city, that I would display an aptitude was never in question. I sat cross-legged on the mat before him and played, gradually stirring to life as I did so, and finally sleep would lift from me like a covering, a smothering that had belonged to the night, till the inner core of my being stood forth and my father could see it clearly – I was a musician, not a maker, but a performer of music, that is what he saw. He taught me all the *ragas,* the *raginis*, and tested my knowledge with rapid, persistent questioning in his unmusical, grating voice. He was unlike my Ustad in every way, for he spat betel juice all down his ragged white beard, he seemed to be aware of everything I did and frequently his hand shot out to grab my ears and pull till I yelped. From such lessons I had a need to escape and, being a small, wily boy, managed this several times a day, slipping through my elders' fingers and hurtling down the steep stairs into the lane where I played *gulli-danda* and *kho* and marbles with the luckier, more idle and less supervised boys of the *mohalla*.

There was a time when I cared more passionately for marbles than for music, particularly a dark crimson, almost black one in which white lines writhed like weeds, or roots, that helped me to win every match I played till the pockets of my *kurta* bulged and tore with the weight of the marbles I won.

How I loved my mother's sweetmeats, too – rather more, I'm sure, than I did the nondescript, mumbling, bald woman who made them. She never came to life for me, she lived some obscure, indoor life, unhealthy and curtained, undemanding and uninviting. But what *halwa* she made, what *jalebis*. I ate them so hot that I burnt the skin off my tongue. I stole my brothers' and sisters' share and was beaten and cursed by the whole family.

Then, when I was older, there was a time when only the cinema mattered. I saw four, five, as many as six cinema shows a week, creeping out of my room at night barefoot, for silence, with money stolen from my father, or mother, or anyone, clutched in my hand, then racing through the night-wild bazaar in time for the last show. Meena Kumari and Nargis were to me the queens of heaven, I put myself in the place of their screen lovers and felt myself grow great, hirsute, active and aggressive as I sat on the straw-stuffed seat, my feet tucked up under me, a cone of salted gram in my hand, uneaten, as I stared at these glistening, sequined queens with my mouth open. Their attractions, their graces filled up the empty spaces of my life and gave it new colours, new rhythms. So then I became aware of the women of our *mohalla* as women: ripe matrons who stood in their doorways, hands on hips, in that hour of the afternoon when life paused and presented possibilities before evening duties choked them off, and the younger girls, always moving, never still, eluding touch. They were like reeds in dirty water for however shabby they were, however unlike the screen heroines, they never quite lacked the enticements of subtle smiles, sly glances and bits of gold braid and lace. Some answered the look in my eyes, prom-

61

ised me what I wanted, later perhaps, after the late show, not now.

But all fell away from me, all disappeared in the shadows, on the side, when I met my Ustad and began to play for him. He took the place of my mother's sweet *halwa*, the cinema heroines, the street beauties, marbles and stolen money, all the pleasures and riches I had so far contrived to extract from the hard stones of existence in my father's house in the music lane. I did not need such toys any more, such toys and dreams. I had found my purpose in life and, by following it without hesitation and without holding back any part of myself, I found such satisfaction that I no longer wished for anything else.

It is true I made a little money on these concert tours of ours, enough to take care of my father during his last years and his illness. I even married. That is, my mother managed to marry me off to some neighbour's daughter of whom she was fond. The girl lived with her. I seldom visited her. I can barely remember her name, her face. She is safe with my mother and does not bother me. I remain free to follow my Ustad and play for him.

I believe he has the same attitude to his family and the rest of the world. At all events I have not seen him show the faintest interest in anything but our music, our concerts. Perhaps he is married. I have heard something of the sort but not seen his wife or known him to visit her. Perhaps he has children and one day a son will appear on stage and be taught to accompany his father. So far it has not happened. It is true that in between tours we do occasionally go home for a few days of rest. Inevitably the Ustad and I both cut short these 'holidays' and return to his house in the city for practice. When I return, he does not question or even talk to me. But when he hears my step, he recognizes it, I know, for he smiles a half-smile, as if mocking himself and me, then he rolls back his muslin sleeve, lifts his *sitar* and nods in my direction. 'The Raga *Desh*,' he may announce, or *'Malhar,'* or *'Megh'* and I sit down behind him, on the bare floor, and play for him the notes he needs for the construction of the raga.

You may think I exaggerate our relationship, his need of me, his reliance on my *tanpura*. You may point out that there are other members of his band who play more important rôles. And I will confess you may be right, but only in a very superficial way. It is quite obvious that the *tabla* player who accompanies him plays an 'important' rôle – a very loud and aggressive, at times thunderous one. But what is this 'importance' of his? It is not indispensable. As even the foremost critics agree, my Ustad is at his best when he is playing the introductory passage, the unaccompanied *alap*. This he plays slowly, thoughtfully, with such purity and sensibility that I can never hear it without tears coming to my eyes. But once Ram Nath has joined in with a tap and a run of his fingers on the *tablas*, the music becomes quick, bold and competitive and, not only in my opinion but also in that of many critics, of diminished value. The audience certainly enjoys the *gat* more than the quiet *alap*, and it pays more attention to Ram Nath than to me. At times he even draws applause for his performance, during a particularly brilliant passage when he manages to match or even outshine my Ustad. Then my Ustad will turn to him and smile, faintly, in approval, or even nod silently for he is so greathearted and generous, my Ustad. He never does this to me. I sit at the back, almost concealed behind my master and his accompanist. I have no solo passage to play. I neither follow my Ustad's raga nor enter into any kind of competition. Throughout the playing of the raga I run my fingers over the three strings of my *tanpura*, again and again, merely producing a kind of drone to fill up any interval in sound, to form a kind of road, or track, for my Ustad to keep to so he may not stray from the basic notes of the raga by which I hold him. Since I never compete, never ask for attention to be diverted from him to me, never try to rival him in his play, I maintain I am his true accompanist, certainly his truer friend. He may never smile and nod in approval of me. But he cannot do without me. This is all the reward I need to keep me with him like a shadow. It does not bother me at all when Ram Nath, who is coarse and hairy and scratches his big stomach under his shirt and wears gold rings in his ears like a washerman, puts out his foot and trips me as I am getting onto the stage, or when I see him helping himself to all the *pulao* on the table and leave me only some cold, unleavened bread. I know his true worth, or lack of it, and merely give him a look that will convey this to him.

Only once was I shaken out of my contentment, my complacency. I am ashamed to reveal it to you, it was so foolish of me. It only lasted a very little while but I still feel embarrassed and stupid when I think of it. It was of course those empty-headed, marble-playing friends of my childhood who led me into it. Once I had put them behind me, I should never have looked back. But they came up to me, after a rehearsal in our home city, a few hours before the concert. They had stolen into the dark hall and sat in the back row, smoking and cracking jokes and laughing in a secret, muffled way which nevertheless drifted up to the stage, distracting those who were not sufficiently immersed in the music to be unaware of the outside world. Of course the Ustad and I never allowed our attention to stray and continued to attend to the music. Our ability to simply shut out all distraction from our minds when we play is a similarity between us of which I am very proud.

As I was leaving the hall I saw they were still standing in the doorway, a jumbled stack of coloured shirts and oiled locks and garish shoes. They clustered around me and it was only because of the things they said, referring to our boyhood games in the alley, that I recognized them. In every other matter they differed totally from me, it was plain to see we had travelled in opposite directions. The colours of their cheap bush-shirts and their loud voices immediately gave me a headache and I found it hard to keep smiling although I knew I ought to be modest and affectionate to them as my art and my position called for such behaviour from me. I let them take me to the tea-shop adjoining the concert hall and order tea for me. For a while we spoke of home, of games, of our families and friends. Then one of them – Ajit, I think – said, 'Bhai, you used to play so well. Your father was so proud of you, he thought you would be a great Ustad. He used to tell us what a great musician you would be one day. What are you doing, sitting at the back of the stage, and playing the tanpura for Rahim Khan?'

No one had ever spoken to me in this manner, in this voice, since my father died. I spilt tea down my lap. My head gave an uncontrolled jerk, I was so shocked. I half-stood up and thought I would catch him by his throat and press till all those ugly words and ugly thoughts of his were choked, bled, white and incapable of moving again. Only I am not that sort of a man. I know myself to be weak, very weak. I only brushed the tea from my clothes and stood there, staring at my feet. I stared at my broken old sandals, streaked with tea, at my loose clothes of white homespun. I told myself I lived so differently from them, my aim and purpose in life were so different from anything those gaudy street vagabonds could comprehend that I should not be surprised or take it ill if there were such a lack of under-standing between us.

'What sort of instrument is the tanpura?' Ajit was saying, still loudly. 'Not even an accompaniment. It is nothing. Anyone could play it. Just three notes, over and over again. Even I could play it,' he ended with a shout, making the others clap his back and lean forwards in laughter at his wit.

Then Bhola leaned towards me. He was the quietest of them, although he wore a shirt of purple and white flowers and had dyed his moustache ginger. I knew he had been to jail twice already for housebreaking and theft. Yet he dared to lean close to me, almost touching me, and to say 'Bhai, go back to the sitar. You even know how to play the sarod and the vina. You could be a great Ustad yourself, with some practice. We are telling you this for your own good. When you become famous and go to America, you will thank us for this advice. Why do you spend your life sitting at the back of the stage and playing that idiot tanpura while someone else takes all the fame and all the money from you?'

It was as if they had decided to assault me. I felt as if they were climbing on top of me, choking me, grabbing me by my hair and dragging me down. Their words were blows, the idea they were throwing at me an assault. I felt beaten, destroyed, and with my last bit of strength shook them off, threw them off and, pushing aside the table and cups and plates, ran out of the tea-shop. I think they followed me because I could hear voices calling me as I went running down the street, pushing against people and only just escaping from under the rickshaws, tongas and buses. It was afternoon, there were crowds on the street, dust and smoke blotted out the natural light of day. I saw everything as vile, as debased, as something amoral and ugly, and pushed it aside, pushed through as I ran.

And all the time I thought, Are they right? Could I have played the sitar myself? Or the sarod, or the vina? And become an Ustad myself? This had never before occurred to me. My father had taught me to play all these instruments and disciplined me severely, but he had never praised me or suggested I could become a front-rank musician. I had learnt to play these instruments as the son of a carpenter would naturally have learnt to make beds and tables and shelves, or the son of a shopkeeper learnt to weigh grain and sell and make money. But I had practised on these instruments and played the ragas he taught me to play without thinking of it as an art or of myself as artist. Perhaps I was a stupid, backward boy. My father always said so. Now these boys who had heard me play in the dark hall of our house in the music lane, told me I could have been an Ustad myself, sat in the centre of the stage, played for great audiences and been applauded for my performance. Were they right? Was this true? Had I wasted my life?

As I ran and pushed, half-crying, I thought these things for the first time in my life, and they were frightening thoughts – large, heavy, dark ones that threatened to crush and destroy me. I found myself pushed up against an iron railing. Holding onto its bars, looking through tears at the beds of flowering cannas and rows of imperial palms of a dusty city park, I hung against those railings, sobbing, till I heard someone address me – possibly a policeman, or a beggar, or perhaps just a kindly passer-by. 'In trouble?' he asked me. 'Got into trouble, boy?' I did not want to speak to anyone and shook him off without looking at him and found the gate and went into the park, trying to control myself and order my thoughts.

I found a path between some tall bushes, and walked up and down here, alone, trying to think. Having cried, I felt calmer now. I had a bad headache but I was calmer. I talked to myself.

When I first met my Ustad, I was a boy of fifteen – a stupid, backward boy as my father had often told me I was. When I walked up to the stage to give him the *tanpura* he had ordered from my father, I saw greatness in his face, the calm and wisdom and kindness of a true leader. Immediately I wished to deliver not only my *tanpura* but my whole life into his hands. Take me, I wanted to say, take me and lead me. Show me how to live. Let me live with you, by you, and help me, be kind to me. Of course I did not say these

67

words. He took the *tanpura* from me and asked me to play it for him. This was his answer to the words I had not spoken but which he had nevertheless heard. 'Play for me' – and with these words he created me, created my life, gave it form and distinction and purpose. It was the moment of my birth and he was both my father and my mother to me. He gave birth to me – Bhaiyya, the *tanpura* player.

Before that I had no life. I was nothing: a dirty, hungry street urchin, knocking about in the lane with other idlers and vagrants. I had played music only because my father made me, teaching me by striking me across the knuckles and pulling my ears for every mistake I made. I had stolen money and sweets from my mother. I was nothing. And no one cared that I was nothing. It was Ustad Rahim Khan who saw me, hiding awkwardly in the shadows of an empty hall with a *tanpura* in my hands, and called me to come to him and showed me what to do with my life. I owe everything to him, my very life to him.

Yes, it was my destiny to play the *tanpura* for a great Ustad, to sit behind him where he cannot even see me, and play the notes he needs so that he may not stray from the bounds of his composition when gripped by inspiration. I give him, quietly and unobtrusively, the materials upon which he works, with which he constructs the great music for which the whole world loves him. Yes, anyone could play the *tanpura* for him, do what I do. But he did not take anyone else, he chose *me*. He gave me my destiny, my life. Could I have refused him? Does a mortal refuse God?

It made me smile to think anyone could be such a fool. Even I, Bhaiyya, had known when the hour of my destiny had struck. Even a backward, feckless boy from the streets had recognized his god when he met him. I could not have refused. I took up the *tanpura* and played for my Ustad, and I have played for him since. I could not 've wished for a finer destiny.

Leaving the park, I hailed a tonga and ordered the driver to take me to my Ustad. Never in my life had I spoken so loudly, as surely as I did then. You should have heard me. I wish my Ustad had heard me.

A Devoted Son

When the results appeared in the morning papers, Rakesh scanned them, barefoot and in his pyjamas, at the garden gate, then went up the steps to the veranda where his father sat sipping his morning tea and bowed down to touch his feet.

'A first division, son?' his father asked, beaming, reaching for the papers.

'At the top of the list, Papa,' Rakesh murmured, as if awed. 'First in the country.'

Bedlam broke loose then. The family whooped and danced. The whole day long visitors streamed into the small yellow house at the end of the road, to congratulate the parents of this *Wunderkind*, to slap Rakesh on the back and fill the house and garden with the sounds and colours of a festival. There were garlands and *halwa*, party clothes and gifts (enough fountain pens to last years, even a watch or two), nerves and temper and joy, all in a multicoloured whirl of pride and great shining vistas newly opened: Rakesh was the first son in the family to receive an education, so much had been sacrificed in order to send him to school and then medical college, and at last the fruits of their sacrifice had arrived, golden and glorious.

To everyone who came to him to say, '*Mubarak*, Varma-*ji*, your son has brought you glory,' the father said, 'Yes, and do you know what is the first thing he did when he saw the results this morning? He came and touched my feet. He bowed down and touched my feet.' This moved many of the women in the crowd so much that they were seen to raise the ends of their saris and dab at their tears while the men reached out for the betel leaves and sweetmeats that were offered around on trays and shook their heads in wonder and approval of such exemplary filial behaviour. 'One does not often see such behaviour in sons any more,' they all agreed, a little enviously perhaps. Leaving the house, some of the women said, sniffing, 'At least on such an occasion they might have served pure *ghee* sweets,' and some of the men said, 'Don't you think old Varma was giving himself airs? He needn't think we don't remember that he comes from the vegetable market himself, his father used to sell vegetables, and he has never seen the inside of a school.' But there was more envy than rancour in their voices and it was, of course, inevitable – not every son in that shabby little colony at the edge of the city was destined to shine as Rakesh shone, and who knew that better than the parents themselves?

And that was only the beginning, the first step in a great, sweeping ascent to the radiant heights of fame and fortune. The thesis he wrote for his M.D. brought Rakesh still greater glory, if only in select medical circles. He won a scholarship. He went to the U.S.A. (that was what his father learnt to call it and taught the whole family to say – not America, which was what the ignorant neighbours called it, but, with a grand familiarity, 'the U.S.A.') where he pursued his career in the most prestigious of all hospitals and won encomiums from his American colleagues which were relayed to his admiring and glowing family. What was more, he came *back*, he actually returned to that small

71

yellow house in the once-new but increasingly shabby colony, right at the end of the road where the rubbish vans tipped out their stinking contents for pigs to nose in and rag-pickers to build their shacks on, all steaming and smoking just outside the neat wire fences and well-tended gardens. To this Rakesh returned and the first thing he did on entering the house was to slip out of the embraces of his sisters and brothers and bow down and touch his father's feet.

As for his mother, she gloated chiefly over the strange fact that he had not married in America, had not brought home a foreign wife as all her neighbours had warned her he would, for wasn't that what all Indian boys went abroad for? Instead he agreed, almost without argument, to marry a girl she had picked out for him in her own village, the daughter of a childhood friend, a plump and uneducated girl, it was true, but so old-fashioned, so placid, so complaisant that she slipped into the household and settled in like a charm, seemingly too lazy and too good-natured to even try and make Rakesh leave home and set up independently, as any other girl might have done. What was more, she was pretty – really pretty, in a plump, pudding way that only gave way to fat – soft, spreading fat, like warm wax – after the birth of their first baby, a son, and then what did it matter?

For some years Rakesh worked in the city hospital, quickly rising to the top of the administrative organization, and was made a director before he left to set up his own clinic. He took his parents in his car – a new, sky-blue Ambassador with a rear window full of stickers and charms revolving on strings – to see the clinic when it was built, and the large sign-board over the door on which his name was printed in letters of red, with a row of degrees and qualifications to follow it like so many little black slaves of the regent. Thereafter his fame seemed to grow just a little

72

dimmer – or maybe it was only that everyone in town had grown accustomed to it at last – but it was also the beginning of his fortune for he now became known not only as the best but also the richest doctor in town.

However, all this was not accomplished in the wink of an eye. Naturally not. It was the achievement of a lifetime and it took up Rakesh's whole life. At the time he set up his clinic his father had grown into an old man and retired from his post at the kerosene dealer's depot at which he had worked for forty years, and his mother died soon after, giving up the ghost with a sigh that sounded positively happy, for it was her own son who ministered to her in her last illness and who sat pressing her feet at the last moment – such a son as few women had borne.

For it had to be admitted – and the most unsuccessful and most rancorous of neighbours eventually did so – that Rakesh was not only a devoted son and a miraculously good-natured man who contrived somehow to obey his parents and humour his wife and show concern equally for his children and his patients, but there was actually a brain inside this beautifully polished and formed body of good manners and kind nature and, in between ministering to his family and playing host to many friends and coaxing them all into feeling happy and grateful and content, he had actually trained his hands as well and emerged an excellent doctor, a really fine surgeon. How one man – and a man born to illiterate parents, his father having worked for a kerosene dealer and his mother having spent her life in a kitchen – had achieved, combined and conducted such a medley of virtues, no one could fathom, but all acknowledged his talent and skill.

It was a strange fact, however, that talent and skill, if displayed for too long, cease to dazzle. It came to pass that the most admiring of all eyes eventually faded and no longer blinked at his glory. Having retired from work and having lost his wife, the old father very quickly went to pieces, as they say. He developed so many complaints and fell ill so frequently and with such mysterious diseases that even his son could no longer make out when it was something of significance and when it was merely a peevish whim. He sat huddled on his string bed most of the day and developed an exasperating habit of stretching out suddenly and lying absolutely still, allowing the whole family to fly around him in a flap, wailing and weeping, and then suddenly sitting up, stiff and gaunt, and spitting out a big gob of betel juice as if to mock their behaviour.

He did this once too often: there had been a big party in the house, a birthday party for the youngest son, and the celebrations had to be suddenly hushed, covered up and hustled out of the way when the daughter-in-law discovered, or thought she discovered, that the old man, stretched out from end to end of his string bed, had lost his pulse; the party broke up, dissolved, even turned into a band of mourners, when the old man sat up and the distraught daughter-in-law received a gob of red spittle right on the hem of her new organza sari. After that no one much cared if he sat up cross-legged on his bed, hawking and spitting, or lay down flat and turned grey as a corpse. Except, of course, for that pearl amongst pearls, his son Rakesh.

It was Rakesh who brought him his morning tea, not in one of the china cups from which the rest of the family drank, but in the old man's favourite brass tumbler, and sat at the edge of his bed, comfortable and relaxed with the string of his pyjamas dangling out from under his fine lawn night-shirt, and discussed or, rather, read out the morning news to his father. It made no difference to him that his father made no response apart from spitting. It was Rakesh, too, who, on returning from the clinic in the evening, persuaded the old man to come out of his room, as bare and desolate as a cell, and take the evening air out in the garden, beautifully arranging the pillows and bolsters on the divan in the corner of the open veranda. On summer nights he saw to it that the servants carried out the old man's bed onto the lawn and himself helped his father down the steps and onto the bed, soothing him and settling him down for a night under the stars.

All this was very gratifying for the old man. What was not so gratifying was that he even undertook to supervise his father's diet. One day when the father was really sick, having ordered his daughter-in-law to make him a dish of *soojie halwa* and eaten it with a saucerful of cream, Rakesh marched into the room, not with his usual respectful step but with the confident and rather contemptuous stride of the famous doctor, and declared, 'No more *halwa* for you, Papa. We must be sensible, at your age. If you must have something sweet, Veena will cook you a little *kheer*, that's light, just a little rice and milk. But nothing fried, nothing rich. We can't have this happening again.'

The old man who had been lying stretched out on his bed, weak and feeble after a day's illness, gave a start at the very sound, the tone of these words. He opened his eyes – rather, they fell open with shock – and he stared at his son with disbelief that darkened quickly to reproach. A son who actually refused his father the food he craved? No, it was unheard of, it was incredible. But Rakesh had turned his back to him and was cleaning up the litter of bottles and packets on the medicine shelf and did not notice while Veena slipped silently out of the room with a little smirk that only the old man saw, and hated.

Halwa was only the first item to be crossed off the old man's diet. One delicacy after the other went – everything fried to begin with, then everything sweet, and eventually everything, everything that the old man enjoyed. The meals that arrived for him on the shining stainless steel tray twice a day were frugal to say the least – dry bread, boiled lentils,

75

boiled vegetables and, if there were a bit of chicken or fish, that was boiled too. If he called for another helping – in a cracked voice that quavered theatrically – Rakesh himself would come to the door, gaze at him sadly and shake his head, saying, 'Now, Papa, we must be careful, we can't risk another illness, you know,' and although the daughter-in-law kept tactfully out of the way, the old man could just see her smirk sliding merrily through the air. He tried to bribe his grandchildren into buying him sweets (and how he missed his wife now, that generous, indulgent and illiterate cook), whispering, 'Here's fifty *paise*' as he stuffed the coins into a tight, hot fist. 'Run down to the shop at the crossroads and buy me thirty *paise* worth of *jalebis*, and you can spend the remaining twenty *paise* on yourself. Eh? Understand? Will you do that?' He got away with it once or twice but then was found out, the conspirator was scolded by his father and smacked by his mother and Rakesh came storming into the room, almost tearing his hair as he shouted through compressed lips, 'Now Papa, are you trying to turn my little son into a liar? Quite apart from spoiling your own stomach, you are spoiling him as well – you are encouraging him to lie to his own parents. You should have heard the lies he told his mother when she saw him bringing back those *jalebis* wrapped up in filthy newspaper. I don't allow anyone in my house to buy sweets in the bazaar, Papa, surely you know that. There's cholera in the city, typhoid, gastro-enteritis – I see these cases daily in the hospital, how can I allow my own family to run such risks?' The old man sighed and lay down in the corpse position. But that worried no one any longer.

There was only one pleasure left the old man now (his son's early morning visits and readings from the newspaper could no longer be called that) and those were visits from elderly neighbours. These were not frequent as his contemporaries were mostly as decrepit and helpless as he and few could walk the length of the road to visit him any more. Old Bhatia, next door, however, who was still spry enough to refuse, adamantly, to bathe in the tiled bathroom indoors and to insist on carrying out his brass mug and towel, in all seasons and usually at impossible hours, into the yard and bathe noisily under the garden tap, would look over the hedge to see if Varma were out on his veranda and would call to him and talk while he wrapped his *dhoti* about him and dried the sparse hair on his head, shivering with enjoyable exaggeration. Of course these conversations, bawled across the hedge by two rather deaf old men conscious of having their entire households overhearing them, were not very satisfactory but Bhatia occasionally came out of his yard, walked down the bit of road and came in at Varma's gate to collapse onto the stone plinth built under the temple tree. If Rakesh were at home he would help his father down the steps into the garden and arrange him on his night bed under the tree and leave the two old men to chew betel leaves and discuss the ills of their individual bodies with combined passion.

'At least you have a doctor in the house to look after you,' sighed Bhatia, having vividly described his martyrdom to piles.

'Look after me?' cried Varma, his voice cracking like an ancient clay jar. 'He – he does not even give me enough to eat.'

'What?' said Bhatia, the white hairs in his ears twitching. 'Doesn't give you enough to eat? Your own son?'

'My own son. If I ask him for one more piece of bread, he says no, Papa, I weighed out the *ata* myself and I can't allow you to have more than two hundred grammes of cereal a day. He *weighs* the food he gives me, Bhatia – he has scales to weigh it on. That is what it has come to.'

'Never,' murmured Bhatia in disbelief. 'Is it possible, even in this evil age, for a son to refuse his father food?'

'Let me tell you,' Varma whispered eagerly. 'Today the family was having fried fish – I could smell it. I called to my daughter-in-law to bring me a piece. She came to the door and said No . . .'

'Said No?' It was Bhatia's voice that cracked. A *drongo* shot out of the tree and sped away. '*No?*'

'No, she said no, Rakesh has ordered her to give me nothing fried. No butter, he says, no oil—'

'No butter? No oil? How does he expect his father to *live?*'

Old Varma nodded with melancholy triumph. 'That is how he treats me – after I have brought him up, given him an education, made him a great doctor. Great doctor! This is the way great doctors treat their fathers, Bhatia,' for the son's sterling personality and character now underwent a curious sea change. Outwardly all might be the same but the interpretation had altered: his masterly efficiency was nothing but cold heartlessness, his authority was only tyranny in disguise.

There was cold comfort in complaining to neighbours and, on such a miserable diet, Varma found himself slipping, weakening and soon becoming a genuinely sick man. Powders and pills and mixtures were not only brought in when dealing with a crisis like an upset stomach but became a regular part of his diet – became his diet, complained Varma, supplanting the natural foods he craved. There were pills to regulate his bowel movements, pills to bring down his blood pressure, pills to deal with his arthritis and, eventually, pills to keep his heart beating. In between there were panicky rushes to the hospital, some humiliating experiences with the stomach pump and enema, which left him frightened and helpless. He cried easily, shrivelling up on his bed, but if he complained of a pain or even a vague, grey fear in the night, Rakesh would simply open another bottle of pills and force him to take one. 'I have my duty to you, Papa,' he said when his father begged to be let off.

'Let me be,' Varma begged, turning his face away from the pills on the outstretched hand. 'Let me die. It would be better. I do not want to live only to eat your medicines.'

'Papa, be reasonable.'

'I leave that to you,' the father cried with sudden spirit. 'Let me alone, let me die now, I cannot live like this.'

'Lying all day on his pillows, fed every few hours by his daughter-in-law's own hands, visited by every member of his family daily – and then he says he does not want to live "like this" ', Rakesh was heard to say, laughing, to someone outside the door.

'Deprived of food,' screamed the old man on the bed, 'his wishes ignored, taunted by his daughter-in-law, laughed at by his grandchildren – *that* is how I live.' But he was very old and weak and all anyone heard was an incoherent croak, some expressive grunts and cries of genuine pain. Only once, when old Bhatia had come to see him and they sat together under the temple tree, they heard him cry, 'God is calling me – and they won't let me go.'

The quantities of vitamins and tonics he was made to take were not altogether useless. They kept him alive and even gave him a kind of strength that made him hang on long after he ceased to wish to hang on. It was as though he were straining at a rope, trying to break it, and it would not break, it was still strong. He only hurt himself, trying.

In the evening, that summer, the servants would come into his cell, grip his bed, one at each end, and carry it out to the veranda, there setting it down with a thump that jarred every tooth in his head. In answer to his agonized complaints they said the Doctor Sahib had told them he must take the evening air and the evening air they would make him take – thump. Then Veena, that smiling, hypocritical pudding in a rustling sari, would appear and pile up the pillows under his head till he was propped up stiffly into a sitting position that made his head swim and his back ache. 'Let me lie down,' he begged. 'I can't sit up any more.'

'Try, Papa, Rakesh said you can if you try,' she said, and drifted away to the other end of the veranda where her transistor radio vibrated to the lovesick tunes from the cinema that she listened to all day.

So there he sat, like some stiff corpse, terrified, gazing out on the lawn where his grandsons played cricket, in danger of getting one of their hard-spun balls in his eye, and at the gate that opened onto the dusty and rubbish-heaped lane but still bore, proudly, a newly touched-up signboard that bore his son's name and qualifications, his own name having vanished from the gate long ago.

At last the sky-blue Ambassador arrived, the cricket game broke up in haste, the car drove in smartly and the doctor, the great doctor, all in white, stepped out. Someone ran up to take his bag from him, others to escort him up the steps. 'Will you have tea?' his wife called, turning down the transistor set, 'or a Coca-Cola? Shall I fry you some *samosas*?' But he did not reply or even glance in her direction. Ever a devoted son, he went first to the corner where his father sat gazing, stricken, at some undefined spot in the dusty yellow air that swam before him. He did not turn his head to look at his son. But he stopped gobbling air with his uncontrolled lips and set his jaw as hard as a sick and very old man could set it.

'Papa,' his son said, tenderly, sitting down on the edge of the bed and reaching out to press his feet.

Old Varma tucked his feet under him, out of the way, and continued to gaze stubbornly into the yellow air of the summer evening.

'Papa, I'm home.'

Varma's hand jerked suddenly, in a sharp, derisive movement, but he did not speak.

'How are you feeling, Papa?'

Then Varma turned and looked at his son. His face was so out of control and all in pieces, that the multitude of expressions that crossed it could not make up a whole and convey to the famous man exactly what his father thought of him, his skill, his art.

'I'm dying,' he croaked. 'Let me die, I tell you.'

'Papa, you're joking,' his son smiled at him, lovingly. 'I've brought you a new tonic to make you feel better. You must take it, it will make you feel stronger again. Here it is. Promise me you will take it regularly, Papa.'

Varma's mouth worked as hard as though he still had a gob of betel in it (his supply of betel had been cut off years ago). Then he spat out some words, as sharp and bitter as poison, into his son's face. 'Keep your tonic – I want none – I want none – I won't take any more of – of your medicines. None. Never,' and he swept the bottle out of his son's hand with a wave of his own, suddenly grand, suddenly effective.

His son jumped, for the bottle was smashed and thick brown syrup had splashed up, staining his white trousers. His wife let out a cry and came running. All around the old man was hubbub once again, noise, attention.

He gave one push to the pillows at his back and dislodged them so he could sink down on his back, quite flat again. He closed his eyes and pointed his chin at the ceiling, like some dire prophet, groaning, 'God is calling me – now let me go.'

81

❧ The Farewell Party ☙

Before the party she had made a list, faintheartedly, and marked off the items as they were dealt with, inexorably – cigarettes, soft drinks, ice, *kebabs* and so on. But she had forgotten to provide lights. The party was to be held on the lawn: on these dry summer nights one could plan a lawn party weeks in advance and be certain of fine weather, and she had thought happily of how the roses would be in bloom and of the stars and perhaps even fireflies, so decorative and discreet, all gracefully underlining her unsuspected talent as a hostess. But she had not realized that there would be no moon and therefore it would be very dark on the lawn. All the lights on the veranda, in the portico and indoors were on, like so many lanterns, richly copper and glowing, with extraordinary beauty as though aware that the house would soon be empty and these were the last few days of illumination and family life, but they did very little to light the lawn which was vast, a still lake of inky grass.

Wandering about with a glass in one hand and a plate of cheese biscuits in another, she gave a start now and then to see an acquaintance emerge from the darkness which had the gloss, the sheen, the coolness but not the weight of water, and present her with a face, vague and without outlines but eventually recognizable. 'Oh,' she cried several times that evening, 'I didn't know you had arrived. I've been looking for you,' she would add with unaccustomed intimacy (was it because of the gin and lime, her second, or because such warmth could safely be held to lead to nothing now that they were leaving town?). The guest, also having had several drinks between beds of flowering balsam and torenias before launching out onto the lawn, responded with an equal vivacity. Sometimes she had her arm squeezed or a hand slid down the bareness of her back – which was athletic: she had once played tennis, rather well – and once someone said, 'I've been hiding in this corner, watching you,' while another went so far as to say, 'Is it true you are leaving us, Bina? How can you be so cruel?' And if it were a woman guest, the words were that much more effusive. It was all heady, astonishing.

It was astonishing because Bina was a frigid and friendless woman. She was thirty-five. For fifteen years she had been bringing up her children and, in particular, nursing the eldest who was severely spastic. This had involved her deeply in the workings of the local hospital and with its many departments and doctors, but her care for this child was so intense and so desperate that her relationship with them was purely professional. Outside this circle of family and hospital – ringed, as it were, with barbed wire and lit with one single floodlight – Bina had no life. The town had scarcely come to know her for its life turned in the more jovial circles of mah-jong, bridge, coffee parties, club evenings and, occasionally, a charity show in aid of the Red Cross. For these Bina had a kind of sad contempt and certainly no time. A tall, pale woman, heavy-boned and sallow, she had a certain presence, a certain dignity, and people, having heard of the spastic child, liked and admired her, but she had not thought she had friends. Yet tonight they were coming forth from the darkness in waves that quite overwhelmed.

Now here was Mrs Ray, the Commissioner's wife, chirping inside a nest of rustling embroidered organza. 'Why are you leaving us so soon, Mrs Raman? You've only been here – two years, is it?'

'Five,' exclaimed Bina, widening her eyes, herself surprised at such a length of time. Although time dragged heavily in their household, agonizingly slow, and the five years had been so hard that sometimes, at night, she did not know how she had crawled through the day and if she would crawl through another, her back almost literally broken by the weight of the totally dependent child and of the three smaller ones who seemed perpetually to clamour for their share of attention, which they felt they never got. Yet now these five years had telescoped. They were over. The Raman family was moving and their time here was spent. There had been the hospital, the girls' school, the boys' school, picnics, monsoons, birthday parties and measles. Crushed together into a handful. She gazed down at her hands, tightened around glass and plate. 'Time has flown,' she murmured incredulously.

'Oh, I wish you were staying, Mrs Raman,' cried the Commissioner's wife and, as she squeezed Bina's arm, her fragrant talcum powder seemed to lift off her chalky shoulders and some of it settled on Bina who sneezed. 'It's been so nice to have a family like yours here. It's a small town, so little to do, at least one must have good friends . . .'

Bina blinked at such words of affection from a woman she had met twice, perhaps thrice before. Bina and her husband did not go in for society. The shock of their first child's birth had made them both fanatic parents. But she knew that not everyone considered this vital factor in their lives, and spoke of 'social duties' in a somehow reproving tone. The Commissioner's wife had been annoyed, she always felt, by her refusal to help out at the Red Cross fair. The hurt silence with which her refusal had been accepted had implied the importance of these 'social duties' of which Bina remained so stubbornly unaware.

However, this one evening, this last party, was certainly given over to their recognition and celebration. 'Oh, everyone, everyone is here,' rejoiced the Commissioner's wife, her eyes snapping from face to face in that crowded aquarium, and, at a higher pitch, cried 'Renu, why weren't you at the mah-jong party this morning?' and moved off into another powdery organza embrace that rose to meet her from the night like a moth and then was submerged again in the shadows of the lawn. Bina gave one of those smiles that easily-frightened people found mocking, a shade too superior, somewhat scornful. Looking down into her glass of gin and lime, she moved on and in a minute found herself brought up short against the quite regal although overweight figure, in raw silk and homespun and the somewhat saturnine air of underpaid culture, of Bose, an employee of the local museum whom she had met once or twice at the art competitions and exhibitions to which she was fond of hauling her children, whether reluctant or enthusiastic, because 'it made a change,' she said.

'Mrs Raman,' he said in the fruity tones of the culture-bent Bengali, 'how we'll miss you at the next children's art competitions. You used to be my chief inspiration—'

'Inspiration?' she laughed, incredulously, spilling some of her drink and proffering the plate of cheese biscuits from which he helped himself, half-bowing as though it were gold she offered, gems.

'Yes, yes, inspiration,' he went on, even more fruitily now that his mouth was full. 'Think of me – alone, the hapless organizer – surrounded by mammas, by primary school teachers, by three, four, five hundred children. And the judges – they are always the most trouble, those judges.

85

And then I look at you – so cool, controlling your children, handling them so wonderfully and with such superb results – my inspiration!'

She was flustered by this unaccustomed vision of herself and half-turned her face away from Bose the better to contemplate it, but could find no reflection of it in the ghostly white bush of the Queen of the Night, and listened to him murmur on about her unkindness in deserting him in this cultural backwater to that darkest of dooms – guardian of a provincial museum – where he saw no one but school teachers herding children through his halls or, worse, Government officials who periodically and inexplicably stirred to create trouble for him and made their official presences felt amongst the copies of the Ajanta frescoes (in which even the mouldy and peeled-off portions were carefully reproduced) and the cupboards of Indus Valley seals. Murmuring commiseration, she left him to a gloomy young professor of history who was languishing at another of the institutions of provincial backwaters that they so deplored and whose wife was always having a baby, and slipped away, still feeling an unease at Bose's unexpected vision of her which did not tally with the cruder reality, into the less equivocal company provided by a ring of twittering 'company wives'.

These women she had always encountered in just such a ring as they formed now, the kind that garden babblers form under a hedge where they sit gabbling and whirring with social bitchiness, and she had always stood outside it, smiling stiffly, not wanting to join and refusing their effusively nodded invitation. They were the wives of men who represented various mercantile companies in the town – Imperial Tobacco, Brooke Bond, Esso and so on – and although they might seem exactly alike to one who did not belong to this circle, inside it were subtle gradations of importance according to the particular company for which each one's husband worked and of these only they themselves were initiates. Bina was, however unwillingly, an initiate. Her husband worked for one of these companies but she had always stiffly refused to recognize these gradations, or consider them. They noted the rather set sulkiness of her silence when amongst them and privately labelled her queer, proud, boring and difficult. Also, they felt she belonged to their circle whether she liked it or not.

Now she entered this circle with diffidence, wishing she had stayed with the more congenial Bose (why hadn't she? What was it in her that made her retreat from anything like a friendly approach?) and was taken aback to find their circle parting to admit her and hear their cries of welcome and affection that did not, however, lose the stridency and harshness of garden babblers' voices.

'Bina, how do you like the idea of going back to Bombay?'

'Have you started packing, Bina? Poor you. Oh, are you having packers over from Delhi? Oh well then it's not so bad.'

Never had they been so vociferous in her company, so easy, so warm. They were women to whom the most awful thing that had ever happened was the screw of a golden ear ring disappearing down the bathroom sink or a mother-in-law's visit or an ayah deserting just before the arrival of guests: what could they know of Bina's life, Bina's ordeal? She cast her glance at the drinks they held – but they were mostly of orange squash. Only the Esso wife, who participated in amateur dramatics and ran a boutique and was rather taller and bolder than the rest, held a whisky and soda. So much affection generated by just orange squash? Impossible. Rather tentatively, she offered them the remains of the cheese biscuits, found herself chirping replies, deploring the nuisance of having packing crates all over the house, talking of the flat they would move into in

Bombay, and then, sweating unobtrusively with the strain, saw another recognizable fish swim towards her from the edge of the liquescent lawn, and swung away in relief, saying, 'Mrs D'Souza! How late you are, but I'm so glad—' for she really was.

Mrs D'Souza was her daughter's teacher at the convent school and had clearly never been to a cocktail party before so that all Bina's compassion was aroused by those school-scuffed shoes and her tea-party best – quite apart from the simple truth that she found in her an honest individuality that all those beautifully dressed and poised babblers lacked, being stamped all over by the plain rubber stamps of their husbands' companies – and she hurried off to find Mrs D'Souza something suitable to drink. 'Sherry? Why yes, I think I'll be able to find you some,' she said, a bit flabbergasted at such an unexpected fancy of the pepper-haired schoolteacher, 'and I'll see if Tara's around – she'll want to see you,' she added, vaguely and fraudulently, wondering why she had asked Mrs D'Souza to a cocktail party, only to see, as she skirted the rose bed, the admirable Bose appear at her side and envelop her in this strange intimacy that marked the whole evening, and went off, light-hearted, towards the table where her husband was trying, with the help of some hired waiters in soggy white uniforms with the name of the restaurant from which they were hired embroidered in red across their pockets, to cope with the flood of drinks this party atmosphere had called for and released.

Harassed, perspiring, his feet burning, Raman was nevertheless pleased to be so obviously employed and be saved the strain of having to converse with his motley assembly of guests: he had no more gift for society than his wife had. Ice cubes were melting on the tablecloth in sopping puddles and he had trouble in keeping track of his bottles: they were, besides the newly bought dozens of beer bottles and Black Knight whisky, the remains of their five years in this town that he now wished to bring to their end – bottles brought by friends from trips abroad, bottles bought cheap through 'contacts' in the army or air force, some gems, extravaganzas bought for anniversaries such as a nearly full bottle of Vat 69, a bottle with a bit of crême de menthe growing sticky at the bottom, some brown sherry with a great deal of rusty sediment, a red Golconda wine from Hyderabad, and a bottle of Remy Martin that he was keeping guiltily to himself, pouring small quantities into a whisky glass at his elbow and gulping it down in between mixing some very weird cocktails for his guests. There was no one at the party he liked well enough to share it with. Oh, one of the doctors perhaps, but where were they? Submerged in grass, in dark, in night and chatter, clatter of ice in glass, teeth on biscuit, teeth on teeth. Enamel and gold. Crumbs and dregs. All awash, all soaked in night. Watery sound of speech, liquid sound of drink. Water and ice and night. It occurred to him that everyone had forgotten him, the host, that it was a mistake to have stationed himself amongst the waiters, that he ought to move out, mingle with the guests. But he felt himself drowned, helplessly and quite delightfully, in Remy Martin, in grass, in a border of purple torenias.

Then he was discovered by his son who galloped through the ranks of guests and waiters to fling himself at his father and ask if he could play the new Beatles record, his friends had asked to hear it.

Raman considered, taking the opportunity to pour out and gulp down some more of the precious Remy Martin. 'All right,' he said, after a judicious minute or two, 'but keep it low, everyone won't want to hear it,' not adding that he himself didn't, for his taste in music ran to slow and melancholy, folk at its most frivolous. Still, he glanced into the lighted room where his children and the children of neighbours and guests had collected, making themselves tipsy on Fanta and Coca-Cola, the girls giggling in a multi-coloured huddle and the boys swaggering around the record-player with a kind of lounging strut, holding bottles in their hands with a sophisticated ease, exactly like experienced cocktail party guests, so that he smiled and wished he had a ticket, a passport that would make it possible to break into that party within a party. It was chillingly obvious to him that he hadn't one. He also saw that a good deal of their riotousness was due to the fact that they were raiding the snack trays that the waiters carried through the room to the lawn, and that they were seeing to it that the trays emerged half-empty. He knew he ought to go in and see about it but he hadn't the heart, or the nerve. He couldn't join that party but he wouldn't wreck it either so he only caught hold of one of the waiters and suggested that the snack trays be carried out from the kitchen straight onto the lawn, not by way of the drawing-room, and led him towards a group that seemed to be without snacks and saw too late that it was a group of the company executives that he loathed most. He half-groaned, then hiccuped at his mistake, but it was too late to alter course now. He told himself that he ought to see to it that the snacks were offered around without snag or error.

Poor Raman was placed in one of the lower ranks of the companies' hierarchy. That is, he did not belong to a British concern, or even to an American-collaboration one, but merely to an Indian one. Oh, a long-established, prosperous and solid one but, still, only Indian. Those cigarettes that he passed around were made by his own company. Somehow it struck a note of bad taste amongst these fastidious men who played golf, danced at the club on Independence Eve and New Year's Eve, invited at least one foreign couple to every party and called their decorative wives 'darling' when in public. Poor Raman never had belonged. It was so obvious to everyone, even to himself, as he passed around those awful cigarettes that sold so well in the market. It had been obvious since their first disastrous dinner party for this very ring of jocular gentlemen, five years ago. Nono had cried right through the party, Bina had spent the evening racing upstairs to see to the babies' baths and bed-time and then crawling reluctantly down, the hired cook had got drunk and stolen two of the chickens so that there was not enough on the table, no one had relaxed for a minute or enjoyed a second – it had been too sad and harrowing even to make a good story or a funny anecdote. They had all let it sink by mutual consent and the invitations to play a round of golf on Saturday afternoon or a rubber of bridge on Sunday morning had been issued and refused with conspiratorial smoothness. Then there was that distressing hobby of Raman's: his impossibly long walks on which he picked up bits of wood and took them home to sandpaper and chisel and then call wood sculpture. What could one do with a chap who did that? He himself wasn't sure if he pursued such odd tastes because he was a social pariah or if he was one on account of this oddity. Not to speak of the spastic child. Now that didn't even bear thinking of, and so it was no wonder that Raman swayed towards them so hesitantly, as though he were wading through water instead of over clipped grass, and handed his cigarettes around with such an apologetic air.

But, after all, hesitation and apology proved unnecessary. One of them – was he Polson's Coffee or Brooke Bond Tea? – clasped Raman about the shoulders as proper men do on meeting, and hearty voices rose together, congratulating him on his promotion (it wasn't one, merely a transfer, and they knew it), envying him his move to the metropolis. They talked as if they had known each other for years, shared all kinds of public schoolboy fun. One – was he Voltas or Ciba? – talked of golf matches at the Willingdon as though he had often played there with Raman, another spoke of *kebabs* eaten on the roadside after a party as though Raman had been one of the gang. Amazed and grateful as a schoolboy admitted to a closed society, Raman nodded and put in a few cautious words, put away his cigarettes, called a waiter to refill their glasses and broke away before the clock struck twelve and the golden carriage turned into a pumpkin, he himself into a mouse. He hated mice.

Walking backwards, he walked straight into the soft barrier of Miss Dutta's ample back wrapped and bound in rich Madras silk.

'Sorry, sorry, Miss Dutta, I'm clumsy as a bear,' he apologized, but here, too, there was no call for apology for Miss Dutta was obviously delighted at having been bumped into.

'My dear Mr Raman, what can you expect if you invite the whole town to your party?' she asked in that piercing voice that invariably made her companions drop theirs self-consciously. 'You and Bina have been so popular – what are we going to do without you?'

He stood pressing his glass with white-tipped fingers and tried to think what he or Bina had provided her with that she could possibly miss. In any case, Miss Dutta could always manage, and did manage, everything single-handedly. She was the town busy-body, secretary and chairman of more committees than he could count: they ranged from the Film Society to the Blood Bank, from the Red Cross to the Friends of the Museum, for Miss Dutta was nothing if not versatile. 'We hardly ever saw you at our film shows of course,' her voice rang out, making him glance furtively over his shoulder to see if anyone were listening, 'but it was so nice *knowing* you were in town and that I could count on you. So few people here *care*, you know,' she went on, and affectionately bumped her comfortable middle-aged body into his as someone squeezed by, making him remember that he had once heard her called

92

a man-eater, and wonder which man she had eaten and even consider, for a moment, if there were not, after all, some charm in those powdered creases of her creamy arms, equalling if not surpassing that of his worn and harassed wife's bony angles. Why did suffering make for angularity? he even asked himself with uncharacteristic unkindness. But when Miss Dutta laid an arm on top of his glass-holding one and raised herself on her toes to bray something into his ear, he loyally decided that he was too accustomed to sharp angles to change them for such unashamed luxuriance, and, contriving to remove her arm by grasping her elbow – how one's fingers sank into the stuff! – he steered her towards his wife who was standing at the table and inefficiently pouring herself another gin and lime.

'This is my third,' she confessed hurriedly, 'and I can't tell you how gay it makes me feel. I giggle at everything everyone says.'

'Good,' he pronounced, feeling inside a warm expansion of relief at seeing her lose, for the moment, her tension and anxiety. 'Let's hear you giggle,' he said, sloshing some more gin into her glass.

'Look at those children,' she exclaimed, and they stood in a bed of balsam, irredeemably crushed, and looked into the lighted drawing room where their daughter was at the moment the cynosure of all juvenile eyes, having thrown herself with abandon into a dance of monkey-like movements. 'What is it, Miss Dutta?' the awed mother enquired. 'You're more up in the latest fashions than I am – is it the twist, the rock or the jungle?' and all three watched, enthralled, till Tara began to totter and, losing her simian grace, collapsed against some wildly shrieking girl friends.

A bit embarrassed by their daughter's reckless abandon, the parents discussed with Miss Dutta whose finger by her own admission, was placed squarely on the pulse of youth, the latest trends in juvenile culture on which Miss Dutta gave a neat sociological discourse (all the neater for having been given earlier that day at the convocation of the Home Science College) and Raman wondered uneasily at this opening of flood-gates in his own family – his wife grown giggly with gin, his daughter performing wildly to a Chubby Checkers record – how had it all come about? Was it the darkness all about them, dense as the heavy curtains about a stage, that made them act, for an hour or so, on the tiny lighted stage of brief intimacy with such a lack of inhibition? Was it the drink, so freely sloshing from end to end of the house and lawn on account of his determination to clear out his 'cellar' (actually one-half of the sideboard and the top shelf of the wardrobe in his dressing-room) and his muddling and mixing them, making up untried and experimental cocktails and lavishly pouring out the whisky without a measure? But these were solid and everyday explanations and there was about this party something out of the ordinary and everyday – at least to the Ramans, normally so austere and unpopular. He knew the real reason too – it was all because the party had been labelled a 'farewell party', everyone knew it was the last one, that the Ramans were leaving and they would not meet up again. There was about it exactly that kind of sentimental euphoria that is generated at a ship-board party, the one given on the last night before the end of the voyage. Everyone draws together with an intimacy, a lack of inhibition not displayed or guessed at before, knowing this is the last time, tomorrow they will be dispersed, it will be over. They will not meet, be reminded of it or be required to repeat it.

As if to underline this new and Cinderella's ball-like atmosphere of friendliness and gaiety, three pairs of neighbours now swept in (and three kochias lay down and died under their feet, to the gardener's rage and sorrow): the couple who lived to the Ramans' left, the couple who lived to their right, and the couple from across the road, all crying, 'So sorry to be late, but you know what a long way we had to come,' making everyone laugh identically at the identical joke. Despite the disparity in their looks and ages – one couple was very young, another middle-aged, the third grandparents – they were, in a sense, as alike as the company executives and their wives, for they too bore a label if a less alarming one: Neighbours, it said. Because they were neighbours, and although they had never been more than nodded to over the hedge, waved to in passing cars or spoken to about anything other than their children, dogs, flowers and gardens, their talk had a vivid immediacy that went straight to the heart.

'Diamond's going to miss you so – he'll be heartbroken,' moaned the grandparents who lived alone in their spotless house with a black labrador who had made a habit of visiting the Ramans whenever he wanted young company, a romp on the lawn or an illicit biscuit.

'I don't know what my son will do without Diamond,' reciprocated Bina with her new and sympathetic warmth. 'He'll force me to get a dog of his own, I know, and how will I ever keep one in a flat in Bombay?'

'When are you going to throw out those rascals?' demanded a father of Raman, pointing at the juvenile revellers indoors. 'My boy has an exam tomorrow, you know, but he said he couldn't be bothered about it – he had to go to the Ramans' farewell party.'

One mother confided to Bina, winning her heart forever, 'Now that you are leaving, I can talk to you about it at last: did you know my Vinod is sweet on your Tara? Last night when I was putting him to bed, he said 'Mama, when I grow up I will marry Tara. I will sit on a white horse and wear a turban and carry a sword in my belt and I will go and marry Tara'. What shall we do about that, eh? Only a ten year difference in age, isn't there – or twelve?' and both women rocked with laughter.

The party had reached its crest, like a festive ship, loud and illuminated for that last party before the journey's end, perched on the dizzy top of the dark wave. It could do nothing now but descend and dissolve. As if by simultaneous and unanimous consent, the guests began to leave (in the wake of the Commissioner and his wife who left first, like royalty) streaming towards the drive where cars stood bumper to bumper – more than had visited the Ramans' house in the previous five years put together. The light in the portico fell on Bina's pride and joy, a Chinese orange tree, lighting its miniature globes of fruit like golden lanterns. There was a babble, an uproar of leavetaking (the smaller children, already in pyjamas, watched openmouthed from a dark window upstairs). Esso and Caltex left together, arms about each other and smoking cigars, like figures in a comic act. Miss Dutta held firmly to Bose's arm as they dipped, bowed, swayed and tripped on their way out. Bina was clasped, kissed – ear rings grazed her cheek, talcum powder tickled her nose. Raman had his back slapped till he thrummed and vibrated like a beaten gong.

It seemed as if Bina and Raman were to be left alone at last, left to pack up and leave – now the good-byes had been said, there was nothing else they could possibly do – but no, out popped the good doctors from the hospital who had held themselves back in the darkest corners and made themselves inconspicuous throughout the party, and now, in the manner in which they clasped the host by the shoulders and the hostess by her hands, and said 'Ah *now* we have a chance to be with you at last, now we can begin *our* party,' revealed that although this was the first time they had come to the Ramans' house on any but professional visits, they were not merely friends – they were almost a part of that self-defensive family, the closest to them in sympathy. Raman and Bina both felt a warm, moist expansion of tenderness inside themselves, the tenderness they had till today restricted to the limits of their family, no farther, as though they feared it had not an unlimited capacity. Now its close horizons stepped backwards, with some surprise.

And it was as the doctors said – the party now truly began. Cane chairs were dragged out of the veranda onto the lawn, placed in a ring next to the flowering Queen of the Night which shook out flounces and frills of white scent with every rustle of night breeze. Bina could give in now to her two most urgent needs and dash indoors to smear her mosquito-bitten arms and feet with Citronella and fetch Nono to sit on her lap, to let Nono have a share, too, in the party. The good doctors and their wives leant forward and gave Nono the attention that made the parents' throats tighten with gratitude. Raman insisted on their each having a glass of Remy Martin – they must finish it tonight, he said, and would not let the waiters clear away the ice or glasses yet. So they sat on the veranda steps, smoking and yawning.

Now it turned out that Dr Bannerji's wife, the lady in the Dacca sari and the steel-rimmed spectacles, had studied in Shantiniketan, and she sang, at her husband's and his colleagues' urging, Tagore's sweetest, saddest songs. When she sang, in heartbroken tones that seemed to come from some distance away, from the damp corners of the darkness where the fireflies flitted,

> 'Father, the boat is carrying me away,
> Father, it is carrying me away from home,'

the eyes of her listeners, sitting tensely in that grassy, inky dark, glazed with tears that were compounded equally of drink, relief and regret.

~ Pigeons at Daybreak ~

One of his worst afflictions, Mr Basu thought, was not to be able to read the newspaper himself. To have them read to him by his wife. He watched with fiercely controlled irritation that made the corners of his mouth jerk suddenly upwards and outwards, as she searched for her spectacles through the flat. By the time she found them – on the ledge above the bathing place in the bathroom, of all places: what did she want with her spectacles in *there*? – she had lost the newspaper. When she found it, it was spotted all over with grease for she had left it beside the stove on which the fish was frying. This reminded her to see to the fish before it was overdone. 'You don't want charred fish for your lunch, do you?' she shouted back when he called. He sat back then, in his tall-backed cane chair, folded his hands over his stomach and knew that if he were to open his mouth now, even a slit, it would be to let out a scream of abuse. So he kept it tightly shut.

When she had finally come to the end of that round of bumbling activity, moving from stove to bucket, shelf to table, cupboard to kitchen, she came out on the balcony again, triumphantly carrying with her the newspaper as well as the spectacles. 'So,' she said, 'are you ready to listen to the news now?'

'Now, he said, parting his lips with the sound of tearing paper, 'I'm ready.'

But Otima Basu never heard such sounds, such ironies or distresses. Quite pleased with all she had accomplished, and at having half an hour in which to sit down comfortably, she settled herself on top of a cane stool like a large soft cushion of white cotton, oiled hair and gold bangles. Humming a little air from the last Hindi film she had seen, she opened out the newspaper on her soft, doughy lap and began to hum out the headlines. In spite of himself, Amul Basu leaned forward, strained his eyes to catch an interesting headline for he simply couldn't believe this was all the papers had to offer.

'"Rice smugglers caught"' she read out, but immediately ran along a train of thought of her own. 'What can they expect? Everyone knows there is enough rice in the land, it's the hoarders and black-marketeers who keep it from us, naturally people will break the law and take to smuggling. . .'

'What else? What else?' Mr Basu snapped at her. 'Nothing else in the papers?'

'Ah – ah – hmm,' she muttered as her eyes roved up and down the columns, looking very round and glassy behind the steel-rimmed spectacles. '"Blue bull menace in Delhi airport can be solved by narcotic drug—"'

'Blue bulls? Blue bulls?' snorted Mr Basu, almost tipping out of his chair. 'How do you mean, "blue bulls"? What's a blue bull? You can't be reading right.'

'I am reading right,' she protested. 'Think I can't read? Did my B.A, helped two children through school and college, and you think I can't read? Blue bulls it says here, blue bulls it is.'

'Can't be,' he grumbled, but retreated into his chair from her unexpectedly spirited defence. 'Must be a printing mistake. There are bulls, buffaloes, bullocks, and *bul-buls*, but whoever heared of a blue bull? Nilgai, do they mean? But that creature is nearly extinct. How can there be any at the airport? It's all rot, somebody's fantasy—'

'All right, I'll stop reading, if you'd rather. I have enough to do in the kitchen, you know,' she threatened him, but he pressed his lips together and, with a little stab of his hand, beckoned her to pick up the papers and continue.

'Ah – ah – hmm. What pictures are on this week, I wonder?' she continued, partly because that was a subject of consuming interest to her, and partly because she thought it a safe subject to move onto. '*Teri Meri Kismet* – "the heartwarming saga of an unhappy wife". No, no, no. *Do Dost* – winner of three Filmfare awards – ahh . . .'

'Please, please, Otima, the news,' Mr Basu reminded her.

'Nothing to interest you,' she said but tore herself away from the entertainments column for his sake. '"Anti-arthritis drug" – not your problem. "Betel leaves cause cancer." Hmph. I know at least a hundred people who chew betel leaves and are as fit—'

'All right. All right. What else?'

'What news are you interested in then?' she flared up, but immediately subsided and browsed on, comfortably scratching the sole of her foot as she did so. '"Floods in Assam." "Drought in Maharashtra." When is there not? "Two hundred cholera deaths." "A woman and child have a miraculous escape when their house collapses." "Husband held for murder of wife." See?' she cried excitedly. 'Once more. How often does this happen? "Husband and mother-in-law have been arrested on charge of pouring kerosene on Kantibai's clothes and setting her on fire while she slept." Yes, that is how they always do it. Why? Probably the dowry didn't satisfy them, they must have hoped to get one more . . .'

He groaned and sank back in his chair. He knew there was no stopping her now. Except for stories of grotesque births like those of two-headed children or five-legged calves, there was nothing she loved as dearly as tales of murder and atrocity, and short of his having a stroke or the fish-seller arriving at the door, nothing could distract her now. He even heaved himself out of his chair and shuffled off to the other end of the balcony to feed the parrot in its cage a green chilli or two without her so much as noticing his departure. But when she had read to the end of that fascinating item, she ran into another that she read out in a voice like a law-maker's, and he heard it without wishing to: '"Electricity will be switched off as urgent repairs to power lines must be made, in Darya Ganj and Kashmere Gate area, from 8 p.m. to 6 a.m. on the twenty-first of May." My God, that is today.'

'Today? Tonight? No electricity?' he echoed, letting the green chilli fall to the floor of the cage where other offered and refused chillies lay in a rotting heap. 'How will I sleep then?' he gasped fearfully, 'without a fan? In this heat?' and already his diaphragm seemed to cave in, his chest to rise and fall as he panted for breath. Clutching his throat, he groped his way back to the cane chair. 'Otima, Otima, I can't breathe,' he moaned.

She put the papers away and rose with a sigh of irritation and anxiety, the kind a sickly child arouses in its tired mother. She herself, at fifty-six, had not a wrinkle on her oiled face, scarcely a grey hair on her head. As smooth as butter, as round as a cake, life might still have been delectable to her if it had not been for the asthma that afflicted her husband and made him seem, at sixty-one, almost decrepit.

'I'll bring you your inhaler. Don't get worried, just don't get worried,' she told him and bustled off to find his inhaler and cortisone. When she held them out to him, he lowered his head into the inhaler like a dying man at the one straw left. He grasped it with frantic hands, almost clawing her. She shook her head, watching him. 'Why do you let yourself get so upset?' she asked, cursing herself for having read

101

out that particular piece of news to him. 'It won't be so bad. Many people in the city sleep without electric fans – most do. We'll manage—'

'*You'll* manage,' he spat at her, 'but I?'

There was no soothing him now. She knew how rapidly he would advance from imagined breathlessness into the first frightening stage of a full-blown attack of asthma. His chest was already heaving, he imagined there was no oxygen left for him to breathe, that his lungs had collapsed and could not take in any air. He stared up at the strings of washing that hung from end to end of the balcony, the overflow of furniture that cluttered it, the listless parrot in its cage, the view of all the other crowded, washing-hung balconies up and down the length of the road, and felt there was no oxygen left in the air.

'Stay out here on the balcony, it's a little cooler than inside,' his wife said calmly and left him to go about her work. But she did it absently. Normally she would have relished bargaining with the fish-seller who came to the door with a *beckti*, some whiskered black river fish and a little squirming hill of pale pink prawns in his flat basket. But today she made her purchases and paid him off rather quickly – she was in a hurry to return to the balcony. 'All right?' she asked, looking down at her husband sunk into a heap on his chair, shaking with the effort to suck in air. His lips tightened and whitened in silent reply. She sighed and went away to sort out spices in the kitchen, to pour them out of large containers into small containers, to fill those that were empty and empty those that were full, giving everything that came her way a little loving polish with the end of her sari for it was something she loved to do, but she did not stay very long. She worried about her husband. Foolish and unreasonable as he seemed to her in his sickness, she could not quite leave him to his agony, whether real or imagined. When the postman brought them a letter from

102

their son in Bhilai, she read out to him the boy's report on his work in the steel mills. The father said nothing but seemed calmer and she was able, after that, to make him eat a little rice and fish *jhol*, very lightly prepared, just as the doctor prescribed. 'Lie down now,' she said, sucking at a fish bone as she removed the dishes from the table. 'It's too hot out on the balcony. Take some rest.'

'Rest?' he snapped at her, but shuffled off into the bedroom and allowed her to make up his bed with all the pillows and bolsters that kept him in an almost sitting position on the flat wooden bed. He shifted and groaned as she heaped up a bolster here, flattened a cushion there, and said he could not possibly sleep, but she thought he did for she kept an eye on him while she leafed through a heap of film and women's magazines on her side of the bed, and thought his eyes were closed genuinely in sleep and that his breathing was almost as regular as the slow circling of the electric fan above them. The fan needed oiling, it made a disturbing clicking sound with every revolution, but who was there to climb up to it and do the oiling and cleaning? Not so easy to get these things done when one's husband is old and ill, she thought. She yawned. She rolled over.

When she brought him his afternoon tea, she asked 'Had a good sleep?' which annoyed him. 'Never slept at all,' he snapped, taking the cup from her hands and spilling some tea. 'How can one sleep if one can't breathe?' he growled, and she turned away with a little smile at his stubbornness. But later that evening he was genuinely ill, choked, in a panic at his inability to breathe as well as at the prospect of a hot night without a fan. 'What will I do?' he kept moaning in between violent struggles for air that shook his body and left it limp. 'What will I do?'

'I'll tell you,' she suddenly answered, and wiped the perspiration from her face in relief. 'I'll have your bed taken up on the terrace. I can call Bulu from next door to do it –

you can sleep out in the open air tonight, eh? That'll be nice, won't it? That will do you good.' She brightened both at the thought of a night spent in the open air on the terrace, just as they had done when they were younger and climbing up and down stairs was nothing to them, and at the thought of having an excuse to visit the neighbours and having a little chat while getting them to come and carry up a string bed for them. Of course old Basu made a protest and a great fuss and coughed and spat and shook and said he could not possibly move in this condition, or be moved by anyone, but she insisted and, ignoring him, went out to make the arrangements.

Basu had not been on the terrace for years. While his wife and Bulu led him up the stairs, hauling him up and propping him upright by their shoulders as though he were some lifeless bag containing something fragile and valuable, he tried to think when he had last attempted or achieved what now seemed a tortuous struggle up the steep concrete steps to the warped green door at the top.

They had given up sleeping there on summer nights long ago, not so much on account of old age or weak knees, really, but because of their perpetual quarrels with the neighbours on the next terrace, separated from theirs by only a broken wooden trellis. Noisy, inconsiderate people, addicted to the radio turned on full blast. At times the man had been drunk and troubled and abused his wife who gave as good as she got. It had been intolerable. Otima had urged her husband, night after night, to protest. When he did, they had almost killed him. At least they would have had they managed to cross over to the Basus' terrace which they were physically prevented from doing by their sons and daughters. The next night they had been even more offensive. Finally the Basus had been forced to give in and retreat down the stairs to sleep in their closed, airless room under the relentlessly ticking ceiling fan. At least it was private there. After the first few restless nights they wondered how they had ever put up with the public sleeping outdoors and its disturbances – its 'nuisance', as Otima called it in English, thinking it an effective word.

That had not – he groaned aloud as they led him up over the last step to the green door – been the last visit he had paid to the rooftop. As Bulu kicked open the door – half-witted he may be, but he was burly too, and good-natured, like so many half-wits – and the city sky revealed itself, in its dirt-swept greys and mauves, on the same level with them, Basu recalled how, not so many years ago, he had taken his daughter Charu's son by the hand to show him the pigeon roosts on so many of the Darya Ganj rooftops, and pointed out to him a flock of collector's pigeons like so many silk and ivory fans flirting in the sky. The boy had watched in silence, holding onto his grandfather's thumb with tense delight. The memory of it silenced his groans as they lowered him onto the bed they had earlier carried up and spread with his many pillows and bolsters. He sat there, getting back his breath, and thinking of Nikhil. When would he see Nikhil again? What would he not give to have that child hold his thumb again and go for a walk with him!

Punctually at eight o'clock the electricity was switched off, immediately sucking up Darya Ganj into a box of shadows, so that the distant glow of Cannaught Place, still lit up, was emphasized. The horizon was illuminated as by a fire, roasted red. The traffic made long stripes of light up and down the streets below them. Lying back, Basu saw the dome of the sky as absolutely impenetrable, shrouded with summer dust, and it seemed to him as airless as the room below. Nikhil, Nikhil, he wept, as though the child might have helped.

Nor could he find any ease, any comfort on that unaccustomed string bed (the wooden pallet in their room was of course too heavy to carry up, even for Bulu). He com-

105

plained that his heavy body sank into it as into a hammock, that the strings cut into him, that he could not turn on that wobbling net in which he was caught like some dying fish, gasping for air. It was no cooler than it had been indoors, he complained – there was not the slightest breeze, and the dust was stifling.

Otima soon lost the lightheartedness that had come to her with this unaccustomed change of scene. She tired of dragging around the pillows and piling up the bolsters, helping him into a sitting position and then lowering him into a horizontal one, bringing him his medicines, fanning him with a palm leaf and eventually of his groans and sobs as well. Finally she gave up and collapsed onto her own string bed, lying there exhausted and sleepless, too distracted by the sound of traffic to sleep. All through the night her husband moaned and gasped for air. Towards dawn it was so bad that she had to get up and massage his chest. When done long and patiently enough, it seemed to relieve him.

'Now lie down for a while. I'll go and get some iced water for your head,' she said, lowering him onto the bed, and went tiredly down the stairs like some bundle of damp washing slowly falling. Her eyes drooped, heavy bags held the tiredness under them.

To her surprise, there was a light on in their flat. Then she heard the ticking of the fan. She had forgotten to turn it off when they went up to the terrace and it seemed the electricity had been switched on again, earlier than they had expected. The relief of it brought her energy back in a bound. She bustled up the stairs. I'll bring him down – he'll get some hours of sleep after all, she told herself.

'It's all right,' she called out as she went up to the terrace again. 'The electricity is on again. Come, I'll help you down – you'll get some sleep in your own bed after all.'

'Leave me alone,' he replied, quite gently.

'Why? Why?' she cried. 'I'll help you. You can get into your own bed, you'll be quite comfortable—'

'Leave me alone,' he said again in that still voice. 'It is cool now.'

It was. Morning had stirred up some breeze off the sluggish river Jumna beneath the city walls, and it was carried over the rooftops of the stifled city, pale and fresh and delicate. It brought with it the morning light, as delicate and sweet as the breeze itself, a pure pallor unlike the livid glow of artificial lights. This lifted higher and higher into the dome of the sky, diluting the darkness there till it, too, grew pale and gradually shades of blue and mauve tinted it lightly.

The old man lay flat and still, gazing up, his mouth hanging open as if to let it pour into him, as cool and fresh as water.

Then, with a swirl and flutter of feathers, a flock of pigeons hurtled upwards and spread out against the dome of the sky – opalescent, sunlit, like small pearls. They caught the light as they rose, turned brighter till they turned at last into crystals, into prisms of light. Then they disappeared into the soft, deep blue of the morning.

Scholar and Gypsy

Her first day in Bombay wilted her. If she stepped out of the air-conditioned hotel room, she drooped, her head hung, her eyes glazed, she felt faint. Once she was back in it, she fell across her bed as though she had been struck by calamity, was extinguished, and could barely bring herself to believe that she had, after all, survived. Sweating, it seemed to her that life, energy, hope were all seeping out of her, flowing down a drain, gurgling ironically.

'But you knew it would be hot,' David said, not being able to help a sense of disappointment in her. He had bought himself crisp bush-shirts of madras cotton and open Kolhapur sandals. He was drinking more than was his habit, it was true, but it did not seem to redden and coarsen him as it did her. He looked so right, so fitting on the Bombay streets, striding over the coconut shells and betel-stained papers and the fish scales and lepers' stumps. 'You could hardly come to India and expect it to be cool, Pat.'

'Hot, yes,' she moaned, 'but not – not *killing*. Not so like death. I feel half-dead, David, sometimes *quite* dead.'

'Shall we go and have a gin-and-lime in the bar?'

She tried that since it seemed to do him so much good. But the bar in the hotel was so crowded, the people there were so large and vital and forceful in their brilliant clothes and with their metallic voices and their eyes that flashed over her like barbers' shears, cutting and exposing, that she felt crushed rather than revived.

David attracted people like a magnet – with his charm, his nonchalance, his grace, he did it so well, so smoothly, his qualities worked more efficiently than any visiting card system – and they started going to parties. It began to seem to her that this was the chief occupation of people in Bombay – going to parties. She was always on the point of collapse when she arrived at one: the taxi invariably stank, the driver's hair dripped oil, and then the sights and scenes they passed on the streets, the congestion and racket of the varied traffic, the virulent cinema posters, the blazing colours of women's clothing, the profusion of toys and decorations of coloured paper and tinsel, the radios and loudspeakers never tuned to less than top volume, and amongst them flower sellers, pilgrims, dancing monkeys and performing bears . . . that there should be such poverty, such disease, such filth, and that out of it boiled so much vitality, such irrepressible life, seemed to her unnatural and sinister – it was as if chaos and evil triumphed over reason and order. Then the parties they went to were all very large ones. The guests all wore brilliant clothes and jewellery, and their eyes and teeth flashed with such primitive lust as they eyed her slim, white-sheathed blonde self, that the sensation of being caught up and crushed, crowded in and choked sent her into corners where their knees pushed into her, their hands slid over her back, their voices bored into her, so that when she got back to the hotel, on David's arm, she was more like a corpse than an American globe-totter.

Folding her arms about her, she muttered at the window, 'I never expected them to be so primitive. I thought it would all be modern, up-to-date. Not this – this wild jungle stuff.'

He was pouring himself a night-cap and splashed it in genuine surprise. 'What do you mean? We've only been seeing the modern and up-to-date. These people would be at home at any New York cocktail party—'

'No,' she burst out, hugging herself tightly. 'No, they would *not*. They haven't the polish, the smoothness, the softness. David, they're *not* civilized. They're still a primitive people. When I see their eyes I see how primitive they are. When they touch me, I feel frightened – I feel I'm in danger.'

He looked at her with apprehension. They had drunk till it was too late to eat and now he was hungry, tired. He found her exhausting. He would have liked to sit back comfortably in that air-conditioned cool, to go over the party, to discuss the people they had met, to share his views with her. But she seemed launched in some other direction, she was going alone and he did not want to be drawn into her deep wake. 'You're very imaginative tonight,' he said lightly, playing with the bottle-opener and not looking at her. 'Here was I, disappointed at finding them so westernized. I would have liked them a bit more primitive – at least for the sake of my thesis. Now look at the Gidwanis. Did you ever think an Indian wife would be anything like Gidwani's wife – what was her name?'

'Oh, she was terrible, terrible,' Pat whispered, shuddering, as she thought of the vermilion sari tied below the navel, of the uneven chocolate-smooth expanse of belly and the belt of little silver bells around it. She didn't care to remember the dance she had danced with David on the floor of the night-club. She had never even looked at the woman's face, she had kept her eyes lowered and not been able to go any further than that black navel. If that was not primitive, what could David, a sociology student, mean by the word?

It was at the Gidwanis' dinner later that week that she

110

collapsed. She had begun to feel threatened, menaced, the moment they entered that flat. Leaving behind them the betel-stained walls of the elevator shaft, the servant boys asleep on mats in the passage, the cluster of watchmen and chauffeurs playing cards under the unshaded bulb in the lobby, they had stepped onto a black marble floor that glittered like a mirror and reflected the priceless statuary that sailed on its surface like ships of stone. Scarlet and vermilion ixora in pots. Menservants in stiffly starched uniform. Jewels, enamel, brocade and gold. Gidwani with a face like an amiable baboon's, immediately sliding a soft hand across her back. His wife's chocolate pudding belly with the sari slipping suggestively about her hips. Pat shrank and shrank. Her lips felt very dry and she licked and licked them, nervously. She lost David's arm. Her feet in their sandals seemed to swell grotesquely. She sat at the table, her head slanting. She saw David looking at her concernedly. The manservant's stomach pushed against her shoulder as he lowered the dishes for her. The dishes smelt, she wondered of what – oil, was it, or goat's meat? It was not conducive to appetite. Her fork slipped. The table slipped. She had fainted. They were all crying, shoving, crowding. She pushed at them with her hands in panic.

'David, get me out, get me out,' she blubbered, trying to free herself of them.

Later, sitting at the foot of her bed, 'We'd better leave,' he said sadly. Was it Gidwani's wife's belly that saddened him, she wondered. It was not a sight that one could forget, or discard, or deny. 'Delhi's said to be dryer,' he said, 'not so humid. It'll be better for you.'

'But your thesis, David?' she wept, repentantly. 'Will you be able to work on it there?'

'I suppose so,' he said gloomily, looking down at her, shrunk into something small on the bed, paler and fainter each day that she spent in the wild jungles of the city of Bombay.

Delhi was dryer. It was dry as a skeleton. Yellow sand seethed and stormed, then settled on wood, stone, flesh and skin, brittle and gritty as powdered bone. Trees stood leafless. Red flowers blazed on their black branches, golden and purple ones burgeoned. Beggars drowsed in their shade, stretched unrecognizable limbs at her. I will pull myself together, Pat said, walking determinedly through the piled yellow dust, I must pull myself together. Her body no longer melted, it did not ooze and seep out of her grasp any more. It was dry, she would hold herself upright, she would look into people's eyes when they spoke to her and smile pleasantly – like David, she thought. But the dust inside her sandals made her feet drag. If she no longer melted, she burnt. She felt the heat strike through to her bones. Even her eyes, protected by giant glare glasses, seemed on fire. She thought she would shrivel up like a piece of paper under a magnifying glass held to reflect the sun. Rubbing her fingers together, she made a scraping, papery sound. Her hair was full of sand.

'But you can't let climate get you down, dear,' David said softly, in order to express tenderness that he hardly felt any longer, seeing her suffer so unbeautifully, her feet dusty, her hair stringy, her face thin and appalled. 'Climate isn't *important*, Pat – rise above it, there's so much *else*. Try to concentrate on *that*.' He wanted to help her. It made things so difficult for him if she wouldn't come along but kept drifting off loosely in some other direction, obliging him to drop things and go after her since she seemed so uncontrolled, dangerously so. He couldn't meet people, work on his thesis, do anything. He had never imagined she could be a burden – not the companion and fellow gypsy she had so fairly promised to be. She came of plain, strong farmer

112

stock – she ought to have some of that blood in her, strong, simple and capable. Why wasn't she capable? He held his hand to her temple – it throbbed hard. They sat sipping iced coffee in a very small, very dark restaurant that smelt, somehow, of railway soot.

'I must try,' she said, flatly and without conviction.

That afternoon she went round the antique shops of New Delhi, determined to take an interest in Indian art and culture. She left the shopping arcade after an hour, horror rising in her throat like vomit. She felt pursued by the primitive, the elemental and barbaric, and kept rubbing her fingers together nervously, recalling those great heavy bosoms of bronze and stone, the hips rounded and full as water-pots, the flirtatious little bells on ankles and bellies, the long, sly eyes that curved out of the voluptuous stone faces, not unlike those of the shopkeepers themselves with their sibilant, inviting voices. Then the gods they showed her, named for her, with their flurry of arms, their stamping feet, their blazing, angered eyes and flying locks, all thunder and lightning, revenge and menace. Scraping the papery tips of her fingers together, she hurried through the dust back to the hotel. Back on her bed, she wept into her pillow for the lost home, for apple trees and cows, for red barns and swallows, for icecream sodas and drive-in movies, all that was innocent and sweet and lost, lost, lost.

'I'm just not sophisticated enough for you,' she gulped over the iced lemon tea David brought her. It was the first time she mentioned the disparity in their backgrounds – it had never seemed to matter before. Laying it bare now was like digging the first rift between them, the first division of raw, red clay. It frightened them both. 'I expect you knew about such things – you must have learnt them in college. You know I only went to high school and stayed home after that—'

'Darling,' he said, with genuine pain and tenderness, and

113

could not go on. His tastes would not allow him to, or his scruples: the vulgarity appalled him as much as the pain. 'Do take a shower and have a shampoo, Pat. We're going out—'

'No, no, no,' she moaned in anguish, putting away the iced tea and falling onto her pillow.

'But to quite different people this time, Pat. To see a social worker – I mean, Sharma's wife is a social worker. She'll show you something quite different. I know it'll interest you.'

'I couldn't bear it,' she wept, playing with the buttons of her dress like a child.

But they did prove different. The Delhi intellectual was poorer than the Bombay intellectual, for one thing. He lived in a small, airless flat with whitewashed walls and a divan and bits of folk art. He served dinner in cheap, bright ceramic ware. Of course there was the inevitable long-haired intellectual – either journalist or professor – who sat cross-legged on the floor and held forth, abusively, on the crassness of the Americans, to David's delight and Pat's embarrassment. But Sharma's wife was actually a new type, to Pat. She was a genuine social worker, trained, and next morning, having neatly tucked the night before under the divan, she took Pat out to see a milk centre, a crèche, a nursery school, clinics and dispensaries, some housed in cow sheds, others in ruined tombs. Pat saw workers' babies asleep like cocoons in hammocks slung from tin sheds on building sites; she saw children with kohl-rimmed eyes solemnly eating their free lunches out of brass containers, and schools where children wrote painstakingly on wooden boards with reed pens and the teacher sneezed brown snuff sneezes at her. It was different in content. It was the same in effect. Her feet dragged, dustier by the hour. Her hair was like string on her shoulders. When she met David in the evening, at the hotel, he was red from the sun, like a well-

114

ripened tomato, longing to talk, to tell, to ask and question, while she drooped tired, dusty, stringy, dry, trying to revive herself, for his sake, with little sips of some iced drink but feeling quite surely that life was shrivelling up inside her. She never spoke of apple trees or barns, of popcorn or drug stores, but he saw them in her eyes, more remote and faint every day. Her eyes had been so blue, now they were fading, as if the memory, the feel of apple trees and apples were fading from her. He panicked.

'We'd better go to the hills for a while,' he said: he did not want murder on his hands. 'Sharma said June is bad, very bad, in Delhi. He says everyone who can goes to the hills. Well, we can. Let's go, Pat.'

She looked at him dumbly with her fading eyes, and tried to smile. She thought of the way the child at the hospital had smiled after the doctor had finished painting her burns with gentian violet and given her a plastic doll. It had been a cheap, cracked pink plastic doll and the child had smiled at it through the gentian violet, its smile stamped in, or cut out, in that face still taut with pain, as by a machine. Pat had known that face would always be in pain, and the smile would always be cut out as by the machine of charity, mechanically. The plastic doll and the gentian violet had been incidental.

At the airlines office, the man could only find them seats on the plane to Manali, in the Kulu Valley. To Manali they went.

Not, however, by plane, for there were such fierce sandstorms sweeping through Delhi that day that no planes took off, and they went the three hundred miles by bus instead. The sandstorm did not spare the highway or the bus – it tore through the cracked windows and buried passengers and seats under the yellow sand of the Rajasthan desert. The sun burnt up the tin body of the bus till it was a

115

great deal hotter inside than out in the sun. Pat sat stone-still, as though she had been beaten unconscious, groping with her eyes only for a glimpse of a mango grove or an avenue of banyans, instinctively believing she would survive only if she could find and drink in their dark, damp shade. David kept his eyes tightly shut behind his glare glasses. Perspiration poured from under his hair down his face, cutting rivers through the map of dust. The woman in the seat behind his was sick all the way up the low hills to Bilaspur. In front of him a small child wailed without stop while its mother ate peanuts and jovially threw the shells over her shoulder into his lap. The bus crackled with sand, peanut shells and explosive sounds from the protesting engine. There was a stench of diesel oil, of vomit, of perspiration and stale food such as he had never believed could exist – it was so thick. The bus was long past its prime but rattled, roared, shook and vibrated all the way through the desert, the plains, the hills, to Mandi where it stopped for a tea-break in a rest house under some eucalyptus trees in which cicadas trilled hoarsely. Then it plunged, bent on suicide, into the Beas river gorge.

After one look down the vertical cliff-side of slipping, crumbling slate ending in the wild river tearing through the narrow gorge in a torrent of ice-green and white spray, David's head fell back against the seat, lolled there loosely, and he muttered 'This is the end, Pat, my girl, I'm afraid it's the end.'

'But it's cooler,' fluted a youthful voice in a rising inflection, and David's head jerked with foolish surprise. Who had spoken? He turned to his wife and found her leaning out of the window, her strings of hair flying back at him in the breeze. She turned to him her excited face – dust-grimed and wan but with its eyes alive and observant. 'I can feel the spray – *cold* spray, David. It's better than a shower or air-conditioning or even a drink. Do just feel it.'

116

But he was too baffled and stunned and slain to feel anything at all. He sat slumped, not daring to watch the bus take the curves of that precarious path hewn through cliffs of slate, poised above the river that hurtled and roared over the black rocks and dashed itself against the mountainside. He was not certain what exactly would happen – whether the overhanging slate would come crashing down upon them, burying them alive, or if they would lurch headlong into the Beas and be dashed to bits on the rocks – but he had no doubt that it would be one or the other. In the face of this certainty, Pat's untimely revival seemed no more than a pathetic footnote.

To Pat, being fanned to life by that spray-spotted breeze, no such possibility occurred. She was watching the white spray rise and spin over the ice-green river and break upon the gleaming rocks, looking out for small sandy coves where pink oleanders bloomed and banana trees hung their limp green flags, exclaiming with delight at the small birds that skimmed the river like foam – feeling curiosity, pleasure and amusement stir in her for the first time since she had landed in India. She no longer heard the retching of the woman behind them or the faint mewing of the exhausted child in front. Peanut shells slipped into her shoes and out of them. The stench of fifty perspiring passengers was lost in the freshness of the mountains. Up on the ridge, if she craned her neck, she could see the bunched needles of pine trees flashing.

When they emerged from the gorge into the sunlight, apricot-warm and mild, of the Kulu valley, she sat back with a contented sigh and let the bus carry them alongside the now calm and wide river Beas, through orchards in which little apples knobbled the trees, past flocks of royal mountain goats and their blanketed shepherds striding ahead with the mountaineer's swing, up into the hills of Manali, its deodar forests indigo in the evening air and the snow-streaked rocks of the Rohtang Pass hovering above them, an incredible distance away.

Then they were disgorged, broken sandals, shells, hair, rags, children and food containers, into the Manali bazaar, and the bus conductor swung himself onto the roof of the bus and hurled down their bags and boxes. David was on his knees, picking up the pieces of his broken suitcase and holding them together. The crying child was fed hot fritters his father had fetched from a wayside food stall. The vomiting woman squatted, holding her head in her hands, and a *pai* dog sniffed at her in curiosity and consolation. A big handsome man with a pigtail and a long turquoise ear-ring came up to Pat with an armful of red puppies, his teeth flashing in a cajoling smile. 'Fifty *rupees*,' he murmured, and raised it to 'Eighty' as soon as Pat reached out to fondle the smallest of them. Touts and pimps, ubiquitously small and greasy, piped around David 'Moonlight Hotel, plumbing and flush toilet,' and 'Hotel Paradise, non-vegetarian and best view, sir.'

David, holding his suitcase in his arms, looked over the top of their heads and at the mountain peaks, as if for succour. Then his face tilted down at them palely and he shook his head, his eyes quite empty. 'Let's go, Pat,' he sighed, and she followed him up through the bazaar for he had, of course, made bookings and they had rooms at what had been described to them as an 'English boarding house.'

It was on the hillside, set in a sea of apple trees, and they had to walk through the bazaar to it, nudging past puppy-sellers, women who had spread amber and coral and bronze prayer bells on the pavement, stalls in which huge pans of milk boiled and steamed and fritters jumped up and hissed, and holiday crowds that stood about eating, talking and eyeing the newcomers.

'Jesus,' David said in alarm, 'the place is full of hippies.'

Pat looked at the faces they passed then and saw that the

118

crowd outside the baker's was indeed one of fair men and women, even if they seemed to be beggars. Some were dressed like Indian gurus, in loincloths or saffron robes, with beads around their necks, others as gypsies in pantaloons or spangled skirts, some in plain rags and tatters. All were barefoot and had packs on their backs, and one or two had silent, stupefied babies astride their hips. 'Why,' she said, watching one woman with a child approach an Indian couple with her empty hand outstretched, 'they might be Americans!' David shuddered and turned up a dusty path that went between the deodar trees to the red-roofed building of the boarding house. But several hippies were climbing the same path, not to the boarding house but vanishing into the forest, or crossing the wooden bridge over the river into the meadows beyond. Americans, Europeans, here in Manali, at the end of the world – what were they doing? she wondered. Well, what was *she* doing? Ah, she'd come to try and live again. She threw back her shoulders and took in lungfuls of the clear, cold air and it washed through her like water, cleansing and pure. Someone in a red cap was sawing wood outside the boarding house, she saw, and blue smoke curled out of its chimney as in a Grandma Moses painting. There was a sound of a rushing stream below. A cuckoo called. Above the tips of the immense deodars the sky was a clear turquoise, an evening colour, without heat although still distilled with sunlight. Dog roses bloomed open and white on the hillside. She tried to clasp David's arm with joy but he was holding onto the suitcase which had broken its locks and burst open and he could not spare her a finger.

'But David,' she coaxed, 'it's going to be lovely.'

'I'm glad,' he said, white-lipped, and pitched the suitcase onto the wooden veranda at the feet of the proprietor who sat benignly as a Buddha on a wooden upright chair, in a white pullover and string cap, gazing down at them with an expression of pity under his bland welcome.

The room was clean, although bare but for two white iron bedsteads and a dressing table with a small yellow mirror. Its window overlooked a yard in which brown hens pecked and climbed onto over-turned buckets and wood piles, and wild daisies bloomed, as white and yellow as fresh bread and butter, around a water pump. The bathroom had no tub but a very well-polished brass bucket, a green plastic mug and, holy of holies, a flush toilet that worked, however reluctantly and complainingly. The proprietor, apple-cheeked and woolly – was he an Anglo-Indian, European or Indian? Pat could not tell – sent them tea and Glaxo biscuits on a tin tray. They sat on the bed and drank the black, bitter tea, sighing 'Well, it's *hot*.'

But Pat could not stay still. Once she had examined the drawers of the dressing table and read scraps from the old newspaper with which they were lined, turned on the taps in the bathroom and washed, changed into her Delhi slippers and drunk her tea, she wanted to go out and 'Explore!' David looked longingly at the clean white, although thin and darned, sheets stretched on the beds and the hairy brown blanket so competently tucked in, but she was adamant.

'We can't waste a minute,' she said urgently, for some unknown reason. 'We mustn't waste this lovely evening.'

He did not see how it would be wasted if they were to lie down on their clean beds, wait for hot water to be brought for their baths and then sleep, but realized it would be somehow craven and feeble for him to say so when she stood at the window with something strong and active in the swing of her hips and a fervour in her newly pink and washed face that he had almost forgotten was once her natural expression – in a different era, a different land.

'We're surrounded by apple trees,' she enticed him, 'and I think, I *think* I heard a cuckoo.'

'Why not?' he grumbled, and followed her out onto the

wooden veranda where the proprietor continued to look comfortable on that upright chair, and down the garden path to the road that took them into the forest.

It was a deodar forest. The trees were so immensely old and tall that while the lower boughs already dipped their feet into the evening, the tops still brushed the late sunlight, and woolly yellow beams slanted through the black trunks as through the pillars of a shadowy cathedral. The turf was soft and uneven under their feet, wild iris bloomed in clumps and ferns surrounded rocks that were conspicuously stranded here and there. Pat fell upon the wild stawberries that grew with a careless luxuriance – small, seed-ridden ones she found sweet. The few people they passed, village men and women wrapped in white Kulu blankets with handsome stripes, had faces that were brown and russet, calm and pleasant, although they neither smiled nor greeted Pat and David, merely observed them in passing. Pat liked them for that – for not whining or wheedling or begging or sneering as the crowds in Bombay and Delhi had done – but simply conferring on them a status not unlike their own. 'Such independence,' she glowed, 'so self-contained. True mountain people, you know.'

David looked at her a little fearfully, not having noted such a surge of Vermont pride in his country wife before. 'Do you feel one of them yourself?' he asked, a little tentatively.

He was startled by the positive quality of the laugh that rang out of her, by the way she threw out her arms in an open embrace. 'Why, *sure*,' she cried, explosively, and sprang over a small stream that ran over the moss like a trickle of mercury. 'Look, here's dear old Jack in the pulpit,' she cried, darting at some ferns from which protruded that rather sinister gentleman, striped and hooded, David thought, like a silent cobra. She plucked it and strode on, her hair no longer like string but like drawn toffee, now catch-

121

ing fire in the sunbeams, now darkening in the shade. After a while, she remarked 'It isn't much like the friendly Vermont woods, really. It's more like a grand medieval cathedral, isn't it?'

'An observation several before you have made on forests,' he remarked, a trifle drily. 'Is one permitted to sit in your cathedral or can one only kneel?' he asked, lowering himself onto a rock. 'Jesus, is my bottom sore from that bus ride.'

She laughed, threw the Jack in the pulpit into his lap and flung herself on the grass at his feet. And so they might have stopped and talked and laughed a bit before going back to an English supper and their fresh, clean beds but, swinging homewards hand-in-hand, they came suddenly upon a strange edifice on a slope in the forest, like a great pagoda built of wood, heavy and dark timber, rough-hewn and sculpted as a stone temple might be, with trees rearing about it in the twilight, shaggy and dark, like Himalayan bears.

'Could it be a temple?' Pat wondered, for the temples she had so far seen had been bursting at the seams with loud pilgrims and busy beggars and priests, affairs of garish paint and plaster, clatter of bells and malodorous marigolds. A still temple in a silent forest – she had quite lost hope of finding such a thing in this overpopulated land.

'We might go in,' David said since she was straining at his hand and, after hovering at the threshold for a bit, they slipped off their sandals and crossed its high wooden plinth.

It was very much darker inside, like a cave scooped out of a tree trunk. The floor, however, was of clay, hard-packed and silky. A shelf of rock projected from the dark wall and a lamp hung from it with a few flowers bright around its wick. It had that minute been blown out by a tall woman with an appropriately wooden face who wore her hair in a tight plait around her head. She lifted her hand, swung only once but vigorously a large bell, and left with a quick stride, barely glancing at them as she went. They bent to study the stone slab beneath the gently smoking lamp and could only just make out the outline of a giant footprint on it. That was all by way of an image and there were neither offerings nor money-box, neither priest nor pilgrim around.

They came out in silence and walked away slowly, as though afraid something would jump out at them from it, or from the forest – they were so much a part of each other, that forest and its temple.

Finally they emerged from the trees and were within sight of the red roof and chimney pot of the English boarding house amongst its apple trees, far below the snow-streaked black ridges of the mountain pass, still pale and luminous against the darkening sky, at once threatening and protective in its attitude, like an Indian god.

'I'm sure I've never seen anything like that before,' Pat murmured then.

'What, not even in Vermont?' he teased, but received no answer.

They ate their dinner in silence, Pat hugely although reflectively, while David sipped a cup of soup and felt as peevish as a neglected invalid.

Perhaps it was only the smallness of Manali – barely a town, merely an overgrown village, a place for shepherds to halt on their way up to the Pass and over it to Lahaul, and apple growers to load their fruit onto lorries bound for the plains, suddenly struck and swollen by a seasonal avalanche of tourists and their vehicles – that led Pat so quickly to know it and feel it as home. It presented no difficulty, as other Indian towns of her acquaintance had, it was innocent and open and if it did not clamorously and cravenly invite, it did not shut its doors either – it had none to shut. It lay in the cup of the valley, the river and forest to one side, bright paddy fields and apple orchards to the other, open and sunlit, small and easy.

She bought herself a cloth bag to sling over her shoulder and with it strode down the single street of Manali in her friendlily squeaking sandals. She stopped at the baker's for ginger biscuits and to smile, somewhat tentitively, at the hippies who stood barefoot at the door, begging for loaves of bread from Indian tourists who seemed as embarrassed as stupefied to discover that it was not only Indians who could beg, and always gave them far more than they did to poorer Indian beggars. She eyed the vegetable stalls and the baskets of ripe fruit on the pavements with envy, wishing she could set up house and do her own marketing. This walk through the bazaar invariably took her to the Tibetan quarter, a smelly lane that took off to one side. Pat could not explain why she had to visit it daily. David refused to accompany her after one visit. He could not face the open drain that one had to jump over in order to enter one of its shops. He could not face the yellow *pai* dogs and the abjectly filthy children one had to pass, nor the extraordinary odour of the shops in which sweaty castaway woollens discarded by returning mountaineers and impecunious hippies made soft furry mountains along with Tibetan rugs, exquisitely chased silver candlesticks and bronze icons that democratically lived together with tawdry plastic and glass jewellery, all presided over by stolid women with faces carved intricately out of hard wood. So David thought them. To Pat they were wise and inscrutable old ladies who parted with objects of great value at pathetically low prices. Pushing through old dresses and woollen pullovers that hung from the rafters, she knelt on worn rugs and shuffled through the baubles and beads in order to pick out a lama carved in wood with the elegance of extreme simplicity, bits of turquoise, a ball of amber like solidified honey, a string of prayer beads as cool as river pebbles between her fingers . . .

'Junk, junk, junk,' David groaned as she spread them out on the bed for him to see. 'Couldn't you walk in some other direction? Must it be that bloody bazaar every day?'

'It isn't,' she protested. 'I walk all over. Just come with me and I'll show you,' she offered, but rather indifferently, and he saw that she did not care at all if he came with her or not, while in Bombay or Delhi she would have cared passionately. This needled him into closing his typewriter, laying his papers in the dressing table drawer and coming with her for once, stepping gingerly over the goat droppings and puddles in the yard, out onto the dusty road.

He found she did know, as she had claimed to, every path and stream and orchard in the place for miles, and was determined to prove it to him. To his horror, she even waved and beamed at the drug-struck, meditative hippies as they swung past the Happy Café where they invariably gathered to eat, talk, play on flutes and gaze into space in that dim, dusty interior where a chart hung on the wall offering the *table d'hôte:* daily it was Brown Rice, Beans and Custard. What hippy had carried his macroculture to Manali, David wondered, pinning it to the wall above the counter where flies circled plates of yellow sweetmeats and Britannia Biscuit packets? The faces of the pale Europeans who gathered there seemed to him distressingly vacant, their postures defeated and vague, but when he mentioned this to Pat, she was scornful.

'You're just making up your mind about them without really looking,' she claimed. 'Now look at that man in white robes – doesn't he look like Christ? And it isn't just the bone structure. And see that young man who's always laughing? That's his pet loris on his shoulder. There's another I see in that bazaar sometimes, who has a pet eagle, but he lives way off in the mountains. It's true they don't talk much – but you often see them laugh. Or else they just sit and think.

Isn't that beautiful, to be able to do that? I think it's beautiful.'

'I think they're stoned,' he said, happy to leave the Happy Café to its shadowy, macrocultural bliss and climb the steep hill into the deodar forest. 'Lord, must we go to the temple *again*?' he moaned, as she led him forward, having already seen it till he could no longer keep his yawns from cracking his jaws apart while he had again to sit outside, on some excruciating roots, and wait for his wife to pay it a ritual visit. He was not really sure what she did in there, nor did he wish to know. Surely she didn't pray? No, she came out looking much too jolly for that.

But no, today she was taking him for a walk and for a walk she would take him, she said, with that new positivism in her jaw-line and swing of her arms that he rather feared. She led him along a stream in which a man and a woman in gypsy dress – and bald patch, and red curls, respectively – were scrubbing some incredibly blackened pots and pans, like children at play – 'Aren't they charming?' Pat enquired, as if of a painted landscape tastefully peopled with just a few rural figures, and David retorted 'Damn vagabonds' – and down lanes that wound through orchards overhung with apricot trees from which fruit dropped ripe and soft onto the stones under their feet, past farm houses screened by daisies and day lilies from which issued bursts, sometimes of tubercular coughing and sometimes of abstract, atonal music, both curiously foreign, and then uphill, beside a stream that leaped over the rocks like a startled hare, white and flashing between ferns and boulders, to a village of large, square stone and wood houses – the ground floors smaller, built solidly of square blocks of stone, the upper floors larger, their elaborately carved wooden balconies overhanging the courtyards in which cows ate the apricots swept up in hills for them, and children climbed crackling haystacks. Apricot trees festooned with unhealthy-looking mistletoe shaded that village and Pat stopped to ask an old man in a blue cap if he had some to sell. They waited in his courtyard, amongst dung pats and milk pails, standing close to the stone wall to let a herd of mountain goats go by, silk-shawled, tip-tapping and bleat-voiced as a party of tipsy ladies, while the man climbed his tree and plucked them a capful. Eating them out of their pockets – they proved not quite ripe and not as sweet as those sold in the bazaar, but Pat wouldn't say so and David did – they continued uphill, out of the village (David glimpsed a lissome brunette in purple robes and Biblical sandals climbing down to the stream but averted his eyes) into the deodar forest again. David was so grateful for its blue shade, and so overfull with bucolic scenes and apricots, that he was ready to sprawl. His wife sprang on ahead, calling, and then he saw her destination. Another temple. He might have known.

Catching up with her, he found Pat fondling the ears of a big tawny dog that had come barking out of the temple courtyard, with familiarity and a wag of its royal tail. 'We can't go in, it's shut,' she reassured him, 'but do see,' she coaxed, and led him through the courtyard and eventually he had to admit that even as Kulu temples went, this one in Nasogi was a pearl. It was no larger than Hansel and Gretel's hut, its roof sloping steeply to the ground, edged with carved icicles of wood. Its doors and beams were massive, but every bit was elegantly carved and fitted. There was a paved courtyard opening into others, all open and inviting, possibly for pilgrims, and around it a grandeur of trees. David lowered himself onto a root, put his arms around his knees, tilted his head to one side and said 'Well yes, you have something here, Pat, I'll give that to you.'

She glowed. 'I think it's most magical spot on earth, if you'd like to know.'

'Aren't you funny?' he commented. 'I take you the length

127

and breadth of India, I show you palaces and museums, jewels and tiger skins – and all the time you were hankering after a forest and an orchard and a village. Little Gretchen you, little Martha, hmm?'

'Do you think that's all I see in it?' she enquired, and he did not quite like, quite trust her sudden gravity that had something too set about it, too extreme, like that of a fanatic. But what was she being so fanatical about – the country life? A mountain idyll? Surely that was obtainable and possible without fanaticism.

She gave only a hint – it was obvious she had thought nothing out yet, however much she had felt. 'This isn't like the rest of India, Dave. It's come to me as a relief, as an escape from India. You know, down in those horrible cities, I'd gotten to think of India as one horrible temple, bursting, *crawling* with people – people on their knees, *hopeless* people – and those horrible idols towering over them with their hundred legs and hundred heads – all *horrible* . . .' (David, tiring of that one adjective, clicked his tongue like an impatient pedagogue, making her veer, only slightly, then return to her track, sifting dry deodar needles through nervous brown fingers) . . . 'and then, to walk through the forest and come upon this – this little shrine – it's like escaping from all those Hindu horrors – it's like coming out into the open and breathing naturally again, without fear. That's what I feel here, you know,' she said with a renewed burst of confidence, '– without *fear*. And you can see that's something I share with, or perhaps have just learnt from, the mountain people here. That's what I admire so in them, in the Tibetans. I don't mean the ones down in the bazaar – those are just like the greasy Indian masses, whining and cajoling and sneering – oh, *horrible* – but the ones one sees on the mountain roads. They're upright, they're honest, independent. They have such a strong swing and a stride to their walk – they walk like gods amongst those crawling, cringing masses. And they haven't those furtive Indian faces either – eyes sliding this way and that, expressions showing and then closing up – *their* faces are all open, and they laugh and sing. All they have is a black old kettle and a pack of wood on their backs, rope sandals and a few sheep, but they laugh and sing and go striding up the mountains like – like lords. I watch them all the time, I admire them, you know, and I got to thinking what makes them so different? I wondered if it was their religion. I feel, being Buddhists, they're different from the Hindus, and it must be something in their belief that gives them this – this fearlessness. When I come to this shrine and sit and think things out quietly, I can see where they get their strength from, and their joy . . .'

But here he could stand it no longer. 'Pat, Pat,' he cried, jumping up and striking his sides. 'You're all confused, Pat, you're so muddled, so hopelessly muddled! My dear, addled wife, Pat!'

She frowned and squinted, her fist closed on a handful of needles, ceased to sift them. 'What do you mean?' she asked, in a tight, closed voice.

'What do I mean? Don't you know? You're sitting outside a *Hindu* shrine, this is a *Hindu* temple, and you're making it out to be a source of Buddhist strength and serenity! Don't you even know that the Kulu Valley has a Hindu population, and the shrines you see here are Hindu shrines?' He whooped with laughter, he pulled her to her feet and dragged her homeward, laughing so much that every time she opened her mouth to protest, he drowned her out with his roars of derision. In the end, that laughter gave him a headache.

He tired of his thesis – the notes he had collected while in Bombay and Delhi and the typescript he was now preparing – long before it was done. The whole job had begun to seem totally irrelevant. Ramming the cover onto the little flat Olivetti, he pushed his legs out so that the waste-paper basket went sprawling, and yawned angrily. The cock on the woodpile at the window caught his eye and gave a wicked wink, but David looked away almost without registering it. Where was Pat?

That was the perennial question these days. Pat was never there. What was more, he no longer asked her where she had been when she appeared for meals or to throw herself down on the bed for the night, her feet raw and dirty from walking in sandals, her cloth bag flung onto the floor. (Once he saw a ragged copy of the Dhammapada slip out of it and hastily looked away: the idea of his poor, addled wife poring over ancient Buddhist texts embarrassed him acutely.) He merely eyed her with accusation and with distaste: she was playing a rôle he had not engaged her to play, she was making a fool of herself, she was embarrassing him, she was absolutely outrageous. As she grew browner from the outdoor life and her limbs sturdier from the exercize, it seemed to him she was losing the fragility, the gentleness that he had loved in her, that she was growing into some tough, sharp countrywoman who might very well carry loads, chop wood, haul water and harvest, but was scarcely fit to be his wife – his, David's, the charming and socially graceful young David of Long Island upbringing – and her movements were marked by rough angles that jarred on him, her voice, when she bothered at all to reply to his vague questions, was brusque and abrupt. It was clear there was no meeting-point between them any more – he would have considered it lowering in status to make a move towards her and she clearly had no interest in meeting him half-way, or anywhere.

He had not cared for the answers she had given him when he had first, mistakenly, asked. On coming upon her one morning, while slouching through the bazaar to post a packet of letters, in, of all places, the Happy Café, round-shouldered on a bench, drinking something cloudy out of a thick glass, in the company of those ragged pilgrims with the incongruously fair heads, he had questioned her with some heat.

'Yes, they're friends of mine,' she shrugged, standing with her new stolidity in the centre of the room to which he had insisted on taking her back. 'I could have told you about them earlier if you'd asked. There's no need for you to spy.'

'Don't be ridiculous,' he snapped. 'Spy on *you*? What for? Why should it interest me what you do with yourself while I'm slogging away in here—'

'Then why ask?' she snapped back.

His curiosity was larger than his distaste in the beginning. Over dinner he asked her the questions he had earlier resolved not to ask and, pleased with the big plateful of food before her, she had talked pleasantly about the Californian couple she had taken up with, and told him the story of their erratic and precipitous voyage from the forests of Big Sur to those of the Kulu Valley, via Afghanistan and Nepal, in search of a guru they had indeed found but now discarded in favour of communal life, vegetarianism and *bhang* which seemed to them a smooth and gentle path to earthly nirvana.

'Nirvana on earth!' he snorted. 'That's a contradiction in terms, don't you know?' Then, seeing her nostrils flare dangerously, went on hastily, but no more wisely, 'Is that what you were drinking down there in that joint, Pat?'

She gave a whoop of delight on seeing the pudding – caramel custard – and buried her nose in a plateful with greed. 'Gee, all this walking makes me hungry,' she apologized, 'and sleepy. Jesus, *how* sleepy.' She went straight to bed.

On another and even more uncomfortable occasion, he had found her while out taking the air after a particularly dull and boring day at the typewriter, in the park in front of

131

the Moonlight Hotel and Rama's Bakery where the hippies were wont to gather, some even to sleep at night, rolled in their blankets on the grass. One of the Indian gurus who held court there was seated, lotus style, under a sun-dressed lime tree, with an admiring crowd of fair and tattered hippies about him, his wife Pat as cross-legged, as smiling and as tattered as the rest. He was too far away to hear what they were saying but it seemed more as if they were bandying jokes – what jokes could East and West possibly share? – than meditating or discoursing on theology. What particularly anguished him was the sight of the Indian tourists who had made an outer cricle around this central core of seekers of nirvana and bliss-through-*bhang*, as if this were one of the sights of the Kulu Valley that they had paid to see. They stood about with incredulous faces, smiling uneasily, exchanging whispered asides with one another, exactly as if they were watching some disquieting although amusing play. There was condescension and, in some cases, pity in their expressions and attitudes that he could not bear to see directed at his fellow fair-heads, much less at his own wife. He turned and almost raced back to the boarding house.

That evening he had tried to question her again but she was tired, vague, merely brushed the hair from her face and murmured 'Yes, that's Guru Dina Nath. He's so sweet – so gay – so –' and went up to bed. He sniffed the air in the room suspiciously. Was it *bhang*? But he wouldn't know what it smelt like if it were. He imagined it would be sweetish and the air in their room was sour, acid. He wrenched the window open, with violence, hoping to wake her. It did not.

The day he gave up questioning her or pursuing her was when she came in, almost prancing, he thought, like some silly mare, burbling, 'Do you remember Nasogi, David? That darling village where we ate apricots? You remember its temple like a little dolls' house? Well, I met some folks

132

who live in a commune right next to it – a big attic over a cow shed actually, but it overlooks the temple and has an orchard all around it, so it's real nice. Edith – she's from Harlem – took me across, and I had coffee with some of them—'

'Sure it was coffee?' he snarled and, turning his back, hurled himself at the typewriter with such frenzy that she could not make herself heard. She sat on her bed, chewing her lip for a while, then got up and went out again. What she had planned to say to him was put away, like an unsuccessful gift.

She kept out of his way after that, and made no further attempts to take him along with her on the way to nirvana. When, at breakfast, he told her, 'It's time I got back to Delhi. I've got more material to research down there and I can't sit here in your valley and contemplate the mountains any more. I plan to book some seats on that plane for Delhi.'

She was shocked, although she made a stout attempt to disguise it, and he was gratified to see this. 'When d'you want to leave?' she asked, spitting a plum seed into her fist.

'Next Monday, I think,' he said.

She said nothing and disappeared for the rest of the day. She was out again before he'd emerged from his bath next morning, and he had to go down to the bus depot by himself, hating every squalid step of the way: the rag market where Tibetans sold stained and soiled imported clothes to avid Indian tourists and played dice in the dust while waiting for customers, the street where snot-gobbed urchins raced and made puppies scream, only just managing to escape from under roaring lorries and stinking buses. He directed looks of fury at the old beggar without a nose or fingers who solicited him for alms and at the pig-tailed Tibetan with one turquoise ear-ring who tried to sell him a mangey pup. 'We're going to get out of here,' he ground out at them through his teeth, and they smiled at him with every encouragement. The booking office was, however, not yet open for business and he was obliged to wait outside the bus depot which was the filthiest spot in the whole bazaar. He stood slouching against a wooden pillar, watching a half-empty bus push through a herd of worriedly bleating sheep and then come up, boiling and steaming, its green-painted, rose-wreathed sides almost falling apart with the effort. It groaned the last few yards of the way and expired at his feet, with a hiss of steam that made its bonnet rise inches into the air.

The driver, a wiry young Sikh who had hung his turban on a peg by the seat and wore only a purple handkerchief over his top-knot, leaped out and raced around to fling open the bonnet before the contraption exploded. His assistant, who had jumped down from the back door and vanished into the nearest shop, a grocer's, now came running out with an enamel jug of water which the driver grabbed from his hands and, before David's incredulous eyes, threw onto the radiator.

The next thing that David knew was that an explosion of steam and boiling water had hit him, hit the driver, the assistant and he didn't know how many bystanders – he couldn't see, he flung his hands to his face, but too late, he was on fire, he was howling – everyone was howling. Someone grabbed his shoulders, someone shouted 'Sir, sir, are you blind? Are you blind?' and he roared 'Yes, damn you, I'm blind, *blind*.' And where was Pat, his bloody useless wife, where was *she*? Here was he, blinded, scalded, being dragged through the streets by strangers, madmen, all trying to carry him, all babbling as at a universal holocaust.

'There, try opening your eyes now. I think you can, son, just try it,' a blessedly American voice spoke, and prised away his hands from his face. In his desperation to see the owner of this blessed voice, David allowed his hands to be loosed from his face and actually opened his eyes – an act he had never thought to perform again – and gazed upon the American doctor with the auburn sideburns and the shirt of blue and brown checked wool as at a vision of St Michael at the golden gates. 'That's wonderful, just wonderful,' beamed the gorgeous man, solid and middle-aged and wondrously square. 'You haven't lost your eyes, see. Now let me just paint those burns for you and you'll leave here as fit as a fiddle, see if you don't . . .' So he burbled on, in that rich, heavy voice from the Middle West, and David sat back as helpless as a baby, and felt those large dry hands with their strong growth of ginger hair gently dab at his face, bringing peace and blessing in their wake. He was the American mission hospital doctor but to David he was God himself on an inspection visit mercifully timed to coincide with David's accident.

It was David's accident. He quite forgot to ask about the driver or his brainless help or the hapless bystanders who had been standing too close to the boiling radiator. He merely sat there, limp and helpless, feeling the doctor's voice flow over him like a stream of American milk. And then he was actually handed a glass of milk – Horlicks, the doctor called it, sweet and hot, and he sipped it with bowed head like a child, afraid he would cry now that the agony was over and the convalescence so sweetly begun.

'It's the shock,' the doctor was saying kindly. 'Your eyes are quite safe, son, and the burns are superficial – luckily – it's just the shock,' and he patted David on the back with those ginger-tufted hands that were so square and sure. 'We see all kinds of accidents up here, you know. Yesterday it was one of those crazy hippies who had to be brought in on a stretcher. He'd fallen off a mountain. Now can you credit that? A grown man just going and falling off a mountain like he was a kid? He'd broken both legs, see. I had to send my assistant with him to Delhi. They'll have quite a time getting him on his feet again but the Holy Family Hospital tries its best. Still,' he added, in the considerate manner of one who knows how to deal with a patient, 'yours sure is the most *unnecessary* accident we've had, I'll say that,' he declared, filling David with sweet pride. Bowing his head, he sipped his milk and drank in the doctor's kindly gossip. He tried to say 'Yeah, those hippies – they shouldn't be allowed – I don't see how they're allowed—' but his voice died away and the doctor shrugged tolerantly and laughed. 'It takes all kinds, you know, but they really are kids, they shouldn't be allowed out of their mamma's sight. How about another drink of Horlicks? You think you can walk home now? Feel okay, son?' David would have given a great deal to say he was not okay at all, that he couldn't possibly walk home, that he wanted to stay and tell the doctor all about Pat, how she had practically deserted him, and about the unsavoury friends she had made here. He wanted to ask him to speak to Pat, reason with her, return his wife to him, return his former life to him. It made him weep, almost, to think that he was expected to get up and walk out. He threw a look of anguish at the doctor as he was seen down the rickety stairs to the bus depot, and did not realize that no one could make out his expression through that coating of gentian violet that coloured his entire face, neck and ears with an extraordinary neon glow.

'My God, what's up with *you*?' screamed Pat when she came in, hours later, and was struck still by shock.

He glared at her, exulting at having elicited such a response from her. But a minute later he saw that she had collapsed against the door frame, not with shock, but with laughter.

'What have you *done*, Dave?' she squealed. 'What made you do *that*?'

Harsh words were exchanged then. David, having lost his tight-lipped control (that morning's sweet Horlicks had washed it away) demanded roughly where she had been when he was standing in the sun to buy tickets and getting scalded and very nearly blinded in the process. Didn't she care about him, he wanted to know, and what *did* she care about at all now? And she, revolted, she said, by his egoism and conceit that didn't allow him to see beyond the tip of his nose – what was wrong with him that he couldn't move out of the way of a bus, for Christ's sake, didn't it just show that he saw nothing, noticed nothing outside himself? – told him what she cared about. She had found a place for herself in the commune at Nasogi. It was what she was meant for, she realized – not going to parties with David, but to live with other men and women who shared her beliefs. They were going to live the simple life, wash themselves and their dishes in a stream, cook brown rice and lentils, pray and meditate in the forest and, at the end, perhaps, become Buddhists – 'A Buddhist, you crackpot? In a Hindu temple?' he spluttered – but she continued calmly that she was sure to find, in the end, something that could not be found on the cocktail rounds of Delhi, Bombay or even, for that matter, Long Island, but that she was positive existed here, in the forest, on the mountains.

'What cocktail rounds? Are you trying to imply I'm a social gadabout, not a serious student of sociology, working on a thesis on which my entire career is based?'

'Working on a thesis?' she screeched derisively. 'Soci-ology? The idea of you, Dave, when you've never so much as looked, I mean really looked, into the soul, the *prana*, of the next man – is just too,—' she spluttered to a stop, wildly threw her hair about her face and burst out 'You, you don't even know it's possible to find Buddha in a Hindu temple. Why, you can find him in a church, a forest, anywhere. Do you think he's as narrow-minded as *you*?' she flung at him, and the explosiveness with which this burst from her showed how his derision had cut into her, how it had festered in her.

The English boarding house was treated to much more hurling of American abuse that night, to throwing around of suitcases, to sounds of packing and dramatic partings and exits, and many heads leant out of the windows into the chalky moonlight to see Pat set off, striding through the daisy-spattered yard in her newly acquired hippy rags that whipped against her legs as she marched off, bag and prayer beads in hand, with never a backward look. There was no one, however, but the proprietor, bland and inscrutable as ever, to see David off next morning making a quieter, neater and sadder departure for Delhi, unconventional only on account of the brilliant purple hue of his face.

If the truth were to be told, he felt greater regret at having to arrive in Delhi with a face like a painted baboon's than to arrive without his wife.